M000208738

Dean Spanley

Books by Lord Dunsany

Novels

The Chronicles of Rodriguez
The King of Elfland's Daughter
The Charwoman's Shadow
The Blessing of Pan
The Curse of the Wise Woman
Up In The Hills
Rory and Bran
My Talks With Dean Spanley
The Story of Mona Sheehy
Guerilla
The Strange Journeys of Colonel Polders
The Last Revolution
His Fellow Men

Short stories

The Gods of Pegana
Time and the Gods
The Sword of Welleran and other stories
The Fortress Unvanquishable, Save for
  Sacnoth
A Dreamer's Tales
The Book of Wonder
Fifty-One Tales
Tales of Wonder
A Dreamer's Tales and other stories
Tales of War
Unhappy Far-Off Things
Tales of Three Hemispheres
Why the Milkman Shudders When He
  Perceives the Dawn
The Travel Tales of Mr. Joseph Jorkens
A City of Wonder
Jorkens Remembers Africa
Jorkens Has a Large Whiskey
The Fourth Book of Jorkens
The Man Who Ate the Phoenix
The Little Tales of Smethers and other
  stories
Jorkens Borrows Another Whiskey
The Sword of Welleran and other tales of
  enchantment

Plays

Five Plays
A Night At An Inn
Plays of Gods and Men
If
The Laughter of the Gods
The Tents of the Arabs
The Queen's Enemies
Plays of Near and Far

Plays of Near and Far (*including* If)
The Compromise of the King of the
  Golden Isles
The Flight of the Queen
Cheezo
A Good Bargain
If Shakespeare Lived Today
Fame and the Poet
The Gods of the Mountain
The Golden Doom
King Argimenes and the Unknown
  Warrior
The Glittering Gate
The Lost Silk Hat
Alexander and Three Small Plays
Alexander
The Old King's Tale
The Evil Kettle
The Amusements of Khan Karuda
Seven Modern Comedies
Atalanta in Wimbledon
The Raffle
The Journey of the Soul
In Holy Russia
His Sainted Grandmother
The Hopeless Passion of Mr. Bunyon
The Jest of Hahalaba
The Old Folk of the Centuries
Lord Adrian
Mr. Faithful
Plays for Earth and Air
Carcassonne

Poetry & Non-fiction

Nowadays
Fifty Poems
If I Were Dictator
Building a Sentence
My Ireland
Patches of Sunlight
Mirage Water
War Poems
Wandering Songs
The Journey
While the Sirens Slept
The Donnellan Lectures
The Sirens Wake
The Year
A Glimpse from a Watch Tower
The Odes of Horace
To Awaken Pegasus

Dean Spanley

MY TALKS WITH DEAN SPANLEY
Lord Dunsany

~

DEAN SPANLEY: THE SCREENPLAY
Alan Sharp

~

Edited by Matthew Metcalfe,
with Chris Smith

HarperCollins*Publishers*

HarperCollins*Publishers*
77–85 Fulham Palace Road,
Hammersmith, London W6 8JB

www.harpercollins.co.uk

This edition published by HarperCollins*Publishers* 2008
1

My Talks With Dean Spanley first published in Great Britain by
William Heinemann Ltd 1936

A catalogue record for this book
is available from the British Library

ISBN: 978 0 00 729045 1

Printed and bound in Great Britain by Clays Ltd, St Ives plc

Mixed Sources
Product group from well-managed
forests and other controlled sources
www.fsc.org Cert no. SW-COC-1806
© 1996 Forest Stewardship Council

FSC is a non-profit international organisation established
to promote the responsible management of the world's forests.
Products carrying the FSC label are independently certified
to assure consumers that they come from forests that are managed
to meet the social, economic and ecological needs
of present and future generations.

Find out more about HarperCollins and the environment at
www.harpercollins.co.uk/green

CONTENTS

My Talks With

Dean Spanley

PREFACE

That there are passages in Dean Spanley's conversation that have sometimes jarred on me, the reader will readily credit. But the more that his expressions have been removed from what one might have expected of a man in his position, or indeed any member of my club, the more they seemed to me to guarantee his sincerity. It would have been easy enough for him to have acted the part that it is his duty to play; but difficult, and I think impossible, to have invented in such meticulous detail the strange story he told me. And for what reason? Upon the authenticity of Dean Spanley's experience I stake my reputation as a scientific writer. If he has deluded me in any particular let scientific bodies reject not only these researches, but any others that I may make hereafter. So sure am I of Dean Spanley's perfect veracity.

Should doubt be expressed of a single page of these talks, and the case against it be made with any plausibility, it is probable that I shall abandon not only this line of research, but that my Investigations into the Origins of the Mentality of Certain Serious Persons, the product of years of observation, may never even be published.

CHAPTER ONE

Were I to tell how I came to know that Dean
Spanley had a secret, I should have to start this tale
at a point many weeks earlier. For the knowledge
came to me gradually; and it would be of little
interest to my readers were I to record the hints
and guesses by which it grew to a certainty. Stray
conversations gradually revealed it, at first partly
overheard from a little group in a corner of a room
at the Olympus Club, and later addressed directly
to myself. And the odd thing is that almost always
it was what Dean Spanley did not say, rather than
any word he uttered, a checking of speech that
occurred suddenly on the top of speculations of
others, that taught me he must be possessed of
some such secret as nobody else, at any rate outside Asia, appears to have any inkling of. If anyone
in Europe has studied the question so far, I gladly

offer him the material I was able to glean from Dean Spanley, to compare and check with his own work. In the East, of course, what I have gathered will not be regarded as having originality.

I will start my story then, on the day on which I became so sure of some astonishing knowledge which Dean Spanley kept to himself, that I decided to act upon my conviction. I had of course cross-examined him before, so far as one can cross-examine an older man in brief conversation in a rather solemn club, but on this occasion I asked him to dine with me. I should perhaps at this point record the three things that I had found out about Dean Spanley: the first two were an interest in transmigration, though only shown as a listener, greater than you might expect in a clergyman; and an interest in dogs. Both these interests were curiously stressed by his almost emphatic silences, just when it seemed his turn to speak upon either of these subjects. And the third thing I chanced to find was that the Dean, though at the club a meagre drinker of wine, was a connoisseur of old port. And it was this third interest of the Dean's that is really the key to the strange information that I am now able to lay before the public. Well then, after many days, during which my suspicions had at first astonished me, and then excitedly ripened, I said to Dean Spanley in the reading-room of the club, 'Of course the difficulty about transmigration is that nobody ever yet remembered having lived a former life.'

'H'm,' said the Dean.

And there and then I asked him if he would dine with me, giving as my reason what I knew to be the only one that would have any chance of bringing him, my wish to have his advice upon some vintage port that had been left me by an aunt, and which had been given to her by Count Donetschau a little before 1880. The port was as good as I had been able to buy, but I doubt if he would have drunk it on that account without any name or history, any more than he would have spoken to a man who was dressed well enough, but who had not been introduced to him.

'Count Donetschau?' he said a little vaguely.

'Count Shevenitz-Donetschau,' I answered.

And he accepted my invitation.

It was a failure, that dinner. I discovered, what I should have known without any experiment, that one cannot make a rather abstemious dean go past the point at which the wit stands sentry over the tongue's utterance, merely by giving him port that he likes. He liked the port well enough, but nothing that I could say made him take a drop too much of it. Luckily I had not given myself away, had not said a word to let him see what I was after. And in a month I tried again. I said I found some port of a different vintage, hidden among the rest, and would value his opinion as to which was the better. And he accepted; and this time I had my plan.

Dinner was light, and as good as my cook could make it. Then came the vintage port, three glasses the same as last time and no more, except for half a glass of the old kind for sake of comparison, and after his three and a half glasses came my plan.

'I have a bottle of imperial Tokay in the cellar,' I said.

'Imperial what!' said the Dean.

'Imperial Tokay,' I said.

'*Imperial* Tokay,' he repeated.

'Yes,' I said. For I had been able to get the loan of one from a friend who in some way had become possessed of half a dozen of this rare wine, that until a little while ago was only uncorked by command of Emperors of Austria. When I say the loan of a bottle, I mean that I had told my friend, who was totally unscientific, that there was something I wanted to draw out of this dean, and that I saw no other way of doing it than to offer him a wine, when he had come to his ordinary limit of drinking, so exciting that he would go further from that point, and that anything left in the bottle, 'after you have made your dean drunk,' as he put it, would be returned to him. I really think that the only reason he gave me the priceless bottle was for a certain unholy joy that his words implied. I doubt if my researches, which without that imperial Tokay would have been impossible, will be of any interest to him. Well, the imperial Tokay was brought in, and I poured out a glass for Dean Spanley. He drank it off at once. I don't know if a dean has a different idea of Heaven, some clearer vision of it, than the rest of us. I shall never know. I can only guess from what I saw in the eyes of Dean Spanley as that imperial Tokay went down.

'Will you have another glass?' I asked.

'I never take more than three glasses usually,' he replied.

'Oh, port doesn't count,' I answered.

He had now had four and a half glasses that evening, and had just come to a point at which such remarks as my last, however silly it may seem here, appear to have wisdom. And, as I spoke, I poured into his glass that curious shining wine, that has somewhat the taste of sherry strangely enchanted. It was now beside him, and we spoke of other things. But when he sipped the Tokay, I said to him rather haltingly, 'I want to ask you about a future life.'

I said it haltingly, because, when two people are speaking, if one of them lacks confidence the other is more apt to assume it. Certainly Spanley did. He replied, 'Heaven. Undoubtedly Heaven.'

'Yes, ultimately of course,' I said. 'But if there were anything in the theories one sometimes hears, transmigration and all that, I was wondering if that might work first.'

There was a certain look of caution yet on his face and, so I went rambling on, rather than leave a silence in which he would have to answer, and by the answer commit himself to concealment of all I wanted to know. 'I mean,' I said, 'going to other lives after this one, animals and all that, and working upwards or downwards in each incarnation, according to whether or not; you know what I mean.'

And then he drained the glass and I poured out another; and, sipping that almost absently, the look of caution went, and I saw instead so beautiful a contentment reigning there in its place, flick-

ering as it seemed with the passage of old reminiscences, that I felt that my opportunity must be
come, and there and then I said to him: 'You see
I've been rather fond of dogs; and, if one chanced
to be one of them in another incarnation, I
wonder if there are any hints you could give me.'

And I seem to have caught the right memory as
it floated by on waves of that wonderful wine, for
he answered at once: 'Always go out of a room first:
get to the door the moment it's opened. You may
not get another chance for a long time.'

Then he seemed rather worried or puzzled by
what he had said, and cleared his throat and
searched, I think, for another topic; but before he
had time to find one I broke in with my thanks,
speaking quickly and somewhat loudly, so as to
frighten his thoughts away from any new topic, and
the thoughts seemed easily guided.

'Thank you very much,' I said, 'very much
indeed. I will say that over and over again to
myself. I will get it into my very; you know, my ego.
And so I shall hope to remember it. A hint like that
will be invaluable. Is there anything more you
could tell me, in case?'

And at the same time, while I spoke to him and
held his attention, I refilled his glass with a hand

that strayed outside the focus of the immediate view of either of us.

'Well,' he said, 'there's always fleas.'

'Yes that of course would be rather a drawback,' I said.

'I wouldn't say that,' he answered. 'I rather like a few fleas; they indicate just where one's coat needs licking.'

And a sudden look came over his face again, as though his thoughts would have strayed where I did not want them, back to strict sobriety and the duller problems of this life. To keep him to the subject that so profoundly interested me I hastily asked his advice, an act which in itself helps to hold the attention of any man.

'How can one best ingratiate oneself, and keep in with the Masters?'

'Ah, the Masters,' he muttered, 'the Great Ones. What benevolence! What wisdom! What power! And there was one incomparably greater and wiser than all of them. I remember how, if he went away for a day, it used to alter the appearance of the whole world; it affected the sunlight; there was less brightness in it, less warmth. I remember how, when he came back, I used to mix myself a good stiff whisky and soda and. . . .'

'But dogs,' I said, 'dogs don't drink whisky.'

I learned afterwards never to interrupt him, but I couldn't help it now, and I wanted to get the truth, and thought he was talking mere nonsense; and yet it wasn't quite.

'Er, er, no,' said Dean Spanley, and fumbled awhile with his memories, till I was afraid I had lost touch with the mystery that I had planned so long to explore. I sat saying never a word. And then he went on again.

'I got the effect,' he said, 'by racing round and round on the lawn, a most stimulating effect; it seems to send the blood to the head in a very exhilarating manner. What am I saying? Dear me, what *am* I saying?'

And I pretended not to have heard him. But I got no more that night. The curtain that cuts us off from all such knowledge had fallen. Would it ever lift again?

CHAPTER TWO

A few nights later I met the Dean at the club. He was clearly vague about what we had talked of when he had dined with me, but just a little uneasy. I asked him then for his exact opinion about my port, until I had established it in his mind that that was my principal interest in the evening we spent together and he felt that nothing unusual could have occurred. Many people would have practised that much deception merely to conceal from a friend that he had drunk a little more wine than he should have; but at any rate I felt justified in doing it now, when so stupendous a piece of knowledge seemed waiting just within reach. For I had not got it yet. He had said nothing as yet that had about it those unmistakable signs of truth with which words sometimes clothe themselves. I dined at the next table to him. He offered me the winelist after he had ordered his port, but I waved it away as I thanked him, and somehow succeeded in conveying to him that I never drank ordinary wines like those. Soon after I asked him if he would care to dine again with me; and he accepted, as I felt sure, for the sake of the Tokay. And I had no Tokay. I had returned the bottle to my friend, and I could not ask for any of that wine from him again. Now I chanced to have met a Maharajah at a party; and, fixing an appointment by telephoning his secretary, I went to see him at his hotel. To put it briefly, I explained to him that the proof of the creed of the Hindus was within my grasp, and that the key to it was imperial Tokay. If he cared to put up the money that would purchase the imperial Tokay, he would receive nothing less than the proof of an important part of his creed. He seemed not so keen as I thought he would be, though whether because his creed had no need of proof, or whether because he had doubts of it, I never discovered. If it were the latter, he concealed it in the end by agreeing to do what I wished; though, as for the money, he said: 'But why not the Tokay?' And it turned out that he had in his cellars a little vault that was full of it. 'A dozen bottles shall be here in a fortnight,' he said.

A dozen bottles! I felt that with that I could unlock Dean Spanley's heart, and give to the Maharajah a strange secret that perhaps he knew already, and to much of the human race a revelation that they had only guessed.

I had not yet fixed the date of my dinner with Dean Spanley, so I rang him up and fixed it with him a fortnight later and one day to spare.

And sure enough, on the day the Maharajah had promised, there arrived at his hotel a box from India containing a dozen of that wonderful wine. He telephoned to me when it arrived, and I went at once to see him. He received me with the greatest amiability, and yet he strangely depressed me; for, while to me the curtain that was lifting revealed a stupendous discovery, to him, it was only too clear, the thing was almost commonplace, and beyond it more to learn than I had any chance of discovering. I recovered my spirits somewhat when I got back to my house with that dozen of rare wine that should be sufficient for twenty-four revelations, for unlocking twenty-four times that door that stands between us and the past, and that one had supposed to be locked for ever.

The day came and, at the appointed hour, Dean Spanley arrived at my house. I had champagne for him and no Tokay, and noticed a wistful expression upon his face that increased all through dinner; until by the time that the sweet was served, and still there was no Tokay, his enquiring dissatisfied glances, though barely perceptible, reminded me, whenever I did perceive them, of those little whines that a dog will sometimes utter when gravely dissatisfied, perhaps because there is another dog in the room, or because for any other reason adequate notice is not being taken of himself. And yet I do not wish to convey that there was ever anything whatever about Dean Spanley that in the least suggested a dog; it was only in my own mind, preoccupied as it was with the tremendous discovery to the verge of which I had strayed, that I made the comparison. I did not offer Dean Spanley any Tokay during dinner, because I knew that it was totally impossible to break down the barrier between him and his strange memories even with Tokay, my own hope being to bring him not so far from that point by ordinary methods, I mean by port and champagne, and then to offer him the Tokay, and I naturally noted the exact amount required with the exactitude of a scientist; my whole investigations depended on that. And then the moment came when I could no longer persuade the Dean to take another drop of wine; of any ordinary wine, I mean; and I put the Tokay before him. A look of surprise came into his face, surprise that a man in possession of Tokay should let so much of the evening waste away before bringing it out. 'Really,' he said, 'I hardly want any more wine, but. . . .'

'It's a better vintage than the other one,' I said, making a guess that turned out to be right.

And it certainly was a glorious wine. I took some myself, because with that great bundle of keys to the mysterious past, that the Maharajah's dozen bottles had given me, I felt I could afford this indulgence. A reminiscent look came over Dean Spanley's face, and deepened, until it seemed to be peering over the boundaries that shut in this life. I waited a while and then I said: 'I was wondering about rabbits.'

'Among the worst of Man's enemies,' said the Dean.

And I knew at once, from his vehemence, that his memory was back again on the other side of that veil that shuts off so much from the rest of us. 'They lurk in the woods and plot, and give Man no proper allegiance. They should be hunted whenever met.'

He said it with so much intensity that I felt sure the rabbits had often eluded him in that other life; and I saw that to take his side against them as much as possible would be the best way to keep his memory where it was, on the other side of the veil; so I abused rabbits. With evident agreement the Dean listened, until, to round off my attack on them, I added: 'And over-rated animals even to eat. There's no taste in them.'

'Oh, I wouldn't say that,' said the Dean. 'A good hot rabbit that has been run across a big field has certainly an, an element of . . .' And he did not complete his sentence; but there was a greedy look in his eyes.

I was very careful about refilling the Dean's glass; I gave him no more for some while. It seemed to me that the spiritual level from which he had this amazing view, back over the ages, was a very narrow one; like a ridge at the top of a steep, which gives barely a resting-place to the mountaineer. Too little Tokay and he would lapse back to orthodoxy; too much, and I feared he would roll just as swiftly down to the present day. It was the ridge from which I feared I had pushed him last time. This time I must watch the mood that Tokay had brought, and neither intensify it nor let it fade, for as long as I could hold it with exactly the right hospitality. He looked wistfully at the Tokay, but I gave him no more yet.

'Rabbits,' I said to remind him.

'Yes, their guts are very good,' he said. 'And their fur is very good for one. As for their bones, if they cause one any irritation, one can always bring them up. In fact, when in doubt always bring anything up: it's easily done. But there is one bit of advice I would give to you. Out-of-doors. It's always best out-of-doors. There are what it is not for us to call prejudices: let us rather say preferences. But while these preferences exist amongst those who hold them, it is much best out-of-doors. You will remember that?'

'Certainly,' I said. 'Certainly.'

And as I spoke I carefully watched his eyes, to see if he was still on that narrow ledge that I spoke of, that spiritual plane from which a man could gaze out on past ages. And he was. A hand strayed tentatively towards the Tokay, but I moved it out of his reach.

'Rats!' I said. And he stirred slightly, but did not seem greatly interested.

And then, without any further suggestion from me, he began to talk of the home-life of a dog, somewhere in England in the days long before motors.

'I used to see off all the carts that drove up to the back-door every day. Whenever I heard them coming I ran round; I was always there in time; and then I used to see them off. I saw them off as far as a tree that there was, a little way down the drive. Always about a hundred barks, and then I used to stop. Some were friends of mine, but I used to see them off the same as the rest. It showed them that the house was well guarded. People that didn't know me used to hit at me with a whip, until they found out that they were too slow to catch me. If one of them ever had hit me I should have seen him off the whole way down the drive. It was always pleasant to trot back to the house from one of these little trips. I have had criticism for this, angry words, that is to say; but I knew from the tone of the voices that they were proud of me. I think it best to see them off like that, because, because. . . .'

I hastily said: 'Because otherwise they might think that the house wasn't properly guarded.'

And the answer satisfied him. But I filled the Dean's glass with Tokay as fast as I could. He drank it, and remained at that strange altitude from which he could see the past.

'Then sooner or later,' he continued, 'the moon comes over the hill. Of course you can take your own line about that. Personally, I never trusted it. It's the look of it I didn't like, and the sly way it moves. If anything comes by at night I like it to come on footsteps, and I like it to have a smell. Then you know where you are.'

'I quite agree,' I said, for the Dean had paused.

'You can hear footsteps,' he went on, 'and you can follow a smell, and you can tell the sort of person you have to deal with, by the kind of smell he has. But folk without any smell have no right to be going about among those that have. That's what I didn't like about the moon. And I didn't like the way it stared one in the face. And there was a look in his stare as though everything was odd and the house not properly guarded. The house was perfectly well guarded, and so I said at the time. But he wouldn't stop that queer look. Many's the time I've told him to go away and not to look at me in that odd manner; and he pretended not to hear me. But he knew all right, he knew he was odd and strange and in league with magic, and he knew what honest folks thought of him: I've told him many a time.'

'I should stand no nonsense from him,' I said.

'Entirely my view,' said the Dean.

There was a silence then such as you sometimes see among well-satisfied diners.

'I expect he was afraid of you,' I said; and only just in time, for the Dean came back as it were with a jerk to the subject.

'Ah, the moon,' he said. 'Yes, he never came any nearer. But there's no saying what he'd have done if I hadn't been there. There was a lot of strangeness about him, and if he'd come any nearer everything might have been strange. They had only me to look after them.

'Only me to look after them,' he added reflectively. 'You know, I've known them talk to a man that ought at least to be growled at; stand at the front door and talk to him. And for what was strange or magical they never had any sense; no foreboding I mean. Why, there were sounds and smells that would make my hair rise on my shoulders before I had thought of the matter, while they would not even stir. That was why they so much needed guarding. That of course was our *raison d'être*, if I may put it in that way. The French often have a way of turning a phrase, that seems somehow more deft than anything that we islanders do. Not that our literature cannot hold its own.'

'Quite so,' I said to check this line of thought, for he was wandering far away from where I wanted him. 'Our literature is very vivid. You have probably many vivid experiences in your own memory, if you cast your mind back. If you cast your mind back, you would probably find material worthy of the best of our literature.'

And he did. He cast his mind back as I told him. 'My vividest memory,' he said, 'is a memory of the most dreadful words that the ears can hear. "Dirty dog." Those unforgettable words; how clear they ring in my memory. The dreadful anger with which they were always uttered; the emphasis, the miraculous meaning! They are certainly the most, the most prominent words, of all I have ever heard. They stand by themselves. Do you not agree?'

'Undoubtedly,' I said. And I made a very careful mental note that, whenever he wandered away from the subject that so much enthralled me, those might be the very words that would call him back.

'Yes, dirty dog,' he went on. 'Those words were never uttered lightly.'

'What used to provoke them?' I asked. For the Dean had paused, and I feared lest at any moment he should find a new subject.

'Nothing,' he said. 'They came as though inspired, but from no cause. I remember once coming into the drawing-room on a lovely bright morning, from a very pleasant heap that there was behind the stable yard, where I sometimes used to go to make my toilet; it gave a very nice tang to my skin, that lasted some days; a mere roll was sufficient, if done in the right place; I came in very carefully smoothed and scented and was about to lie down in a lovely patch of sunlight, when these dreadful words broke out. They used to come like lightning, like thunder and lightning together. There was no cause for them; they were just inspired.'

He was silent, reflecting sadly. And before his reflections could change I said, 'What did you do?'

'I just slunk out,' he said. 'There was nothing else to do. I slunk out and rolled in ordinary grass and humbled myself, and came back later with my fur all rough and untidy and that lovely aroma gone, just a common dog. I came back and knocked at the door and put my head in, when the door was opened at last, and kept it very low, and my tail low too, and I came in very slowly; and they looked at me, holding their anger back by the collar; and I went slower still, and they stood over

me and stooped; and then in the end they did not
let their anger loose, and I hid in a corner I knew
of. Dirty dog. Yes, yes. There are few words more
terrible.'

The Dean then fell into a reverie, till presently
there came the same look of confusion, and even
alarm, on his face, that I had noticed once before,
when he had suddenly cried out, 'What am I talking about?' And to forestall any such uncomfortable perplexity I began to talk myself. 'The
lighting, the upkeep and the culinary problems,' I
said, 'are on the one hand. On the other, the
Committee should so manage the club that its
amenities are available to all, or even more so. You,
no doubt, agree there.'

'Eh?' he said. 'Oh yes, yes.'

I tried no more that night, and the rest of our
conversation was of this world, and of this immediate sojourn.

CHAPTER THREE

'I was the hell of a dog,' said the Dean, when next I was able to tempt him with the Tokay to that eminence of the mind from which he had this remarkable view down the ages; but it was not easily done, in fact it took me several weeks. 'A hell of a dog. I had often to growl so as to warn people. I used to wag my tail at the same time, so as to let them know that I was only meaning to warn them, and they should not think I was angry. Sometimes I used to scratch up the earth, merely to feel my strength and to know that I was stronger than the earth, but I never went on long enough to harm it. Other dogs never dared do more than threaten me; I seldom had to bite them, my growl was enough, and a certain look that I had on my face and teeth, and my magnificent size, which increased when I was angry, so that they could see how large I really was.

'They were lucky to have me guard them. It was an inestimable privilege to serve them; they had unearthly wisdom; but . . .'

'But they needed guarding,' I said. For I remembered this mood of his. And my words kept him to it.

'They needed it,' he said. 'One night I remember a fox came quite near to the house and barked at them. Came out of the woods and on to our lawn and barked. You can't have that sort of thing. There's no greater enemy of Man than the fox. They didn't know that. They hunted him now and then for sport; but they never knew what an enemy he was. I knew. They never knew that he has no reverence for Man, and no respect for his chickens. I knew. They never knew of his plots. And here he was on the lawn barking at men. I was unfortunately in the drawing-room, and the doors were shut, or my vengeance would have been frightful. I should have gone out and leapt on him, probably in one single bound from the hall door, and I should have torn him up into four or five pieces and eaten every one of them. And that is just what I told him, holding back nothing. And then I told him all over again. Somebody had to tell him.

'Then one of the Wise Ones came and told me not to make so much noise; and out of respect to him I stopped. But when he went away the fox was still within hearing, so I told him about it again. It was better to tell him again, so as to make quite sure. And so I guarded the house against all manner of dangers and insults, of which their miraculous wisdom had never taken account.'

'What other dangers?' I asked. For the Dean was looking rather observantly at objects on the table, peering at them from under his thick eyebrows, so that in a few moments his consciousness would have been definitely in the world of the outer eye, and far away from the age that has gone from us.

'Dangers?' he said.

'Yes,' I replied.

'The dark of the woods,' he answered, 'and the mystery of night. There lurked things there of which Man himself knew nothing, and even I could only guess.'

'How did you guess?' I asked him.

'By smells and little sounds,' said the Dean.

It was this remark about the woods and the night, and the eager way in which he spoke of the smells and the sounds, that first made me sure that the Dean was speaking from knowledge, and that he really had known another life in a strangely different body. Why these words made me sure I cannot say; I can only say that it is oddly often the case that some quite trivial remark in a man's conversation will suddenly make you sure that he knows what he is talking about. A man will be talking perhaps about pictures, and all at once he will make you feel that Raphael, for instance, is real to him, and that he is not merely making conversation. In the same way I felt, I can hardly say why, that the woods were real to the Dean, and the work of a dog no less to him than an avocation. I do not think I have explained how I came to be sure of this, but from that moment any scientific interest in what my Tokay was revealing was surpassed by a private anxiety to gather what hints I could for my own ends. I did not like to be adrift as I was in a world in which transmigration must be recognised as a fact, without the faintest idea of the kind of problems with which one would have to deal, if one should suddenly find oneself a dog, in what was very likely an English rectory. That possibility came on me with more suddenness than it probably does to my reader, to whom I am breaking it perhaps more gently. From now on I was no longer probing a man's eccentric experience, so much as looking to him for advice. Whether it is possible to carry any such advice forward to the time one might need it is doubtful, but I mean to try my best by committing it carefully to memory, and all that I gleaned from the Dean is of course at my reader's disposal. I asked him first about the simple things; food, water and sleep. I remember particularly his advice about sleep, probably because it confused me and so made me think; but, whatever the cause, it is particularly clear in my memory. 'You should always pull up your blanket over your lips,' he said. 'It ensures warm air when you sleep, and it is very important.'

It was some time since he had had a glass of Tokay, and to have questioned him as to his meaning would at once have induced in him a logical, or reasonable, frame of mind. We boast so much of our reason, but what can it see compared to that view down the ages that was now being laid before me? It is blind, compared to the Dean.

Luckily I did not have to question him, for by a little flash of memory I recalled a dog sleeping, a certain spaniel I knew; and I remembered how he always tucked the feathery end of his tail over his nostrils in preparation for going to sleep; he belonged to an ignorant man who had neglected to have his tail cut off as a puppy. It was a tail that the Dean meant, not a blanket.

Clear though the meaning was to me the moment I thought of the spaniel, I saw that the confusion of the Dean's remark could only mean that a mist was beginning to gather over his view of time, and I hastily filled his glass. I watched anxiously till he drank it; it must have been his third or fourth; and soon I saw from the clearness of his phrases, and a greater strength in all his utterances, that he was safely back again looking out over clear years.

'The Wise Ones, the Great Ones,' he went on meditatively, 'they give you straw. But they do not, of course, make your bed for you. I trust one can do that. One does it, you know, by walking round several times, the oftener the better. The more you walk round, the better your bed fits you.'

I could see from the way he spoke that the Dean was speaking the truth. After all, I had made no new discovery. In *vino veritas*; that was all. Though the boundaries of this adage had been extended by my talks with Dean Spanley, beyond, I suppose, any limits previously known to man; at any rate this side of Asia.

'Clean straw is bad,' continued the Dean; 'because there is no flavour to it. No.'

He was meditating again, and I let him meditate,

leaving him to bring up out of that strange past whatever he would for me.

'If you find anything good, hide it,' he continued. 'The world is full of others; and they all seem to get to know, if you have found anything good. It is best therefore to bury it. And to bury it when no one is looking on. And to smooth everything over it. Anything good always improves with keeping a few days. And you know it's always there when you want it. I have sometimes smoothed things over it so carefully that I have been unable to find it when requiring it, but the feeling that it's there always remains. It is a very pleasant feeling, hard to describe. Those buryings represent wealth, which of course is a feeling denied to those greedy fellows who eat every bone they find, the moment they find it. I have even buried a bone when I've been hungry, for the pleasure of knowing that it was there. What am I saying! Oh Heavens, what am I saying!'

So sudden, so unexpected was this rush back down the ages, and just when I thought that he had had ample Tokay, that I scarcely knew what to do. But, whatever I did, it had to be done instantly; and at all costs I had to preserve from the Dean the secret that through his babblings I was tapping a source of knowledge that was new to this side of the world, for I knew instinctively that he would have put a stop to it. He had uttered once before in my hearing a similar exclamation, but not with anything like the shocked intensity with which he was now vibrating, and his agitation seemed even about to increase. I had, as I say, to act instantly. What I did made a certain coldness between me and the Dean, that lasted unfortunately for several weeks, but at least I preserved the secret. I fell forward over the table and lay unconscious, as though overcome by Tokay.

CHAPTER FOUR

There was one advantage in the awkwardness that I felt when I next saw the Dean at the club, and that was that my obvious embarrassment attracted his attention away from the direction in which a single wandering thought might have ruined everything. It was of vital importance to my researches that any question about over-indulgence in a rare wine should be directed solely at me. My embarrassment was not feigned, but there was no need to conceal it. I passed him by one day rather sheepishly as I crossed the main hall of the club and saw him standing there looking rather large. I knew he would not give me away to the other members, nor quite condone my lapse. And then one day I very humbly apologised to him in the reading-room.

'That Tokay,' I said. 'I am afraid it may have been a little stronger than I thought.'

'Not at all,' said the Dean.

And I think we both felt better after that; I for having made my apology, he for the generosity with which his few kind words had bestowed forgiveness. But it was some while before I felt that I could quite ask him to dine with me. Much roundabout talk about the different dates and vintages of imperial Tokay took place before I could bring myself to do that; but in the end I did, and so Dean Spanley and I sat down to dinner again.

Now I don't want to take credit for things that I have not done, and I will not claim that I manoeuvred my guest to take up a certain attitude; I think it was merely due to a mood of the Dean. But certainly what happened was that the Dean took up a broad and tolerant line and drank his Tokay like a man, with the implication made clear, in spite of his silence, that there was no harm in Tokay, but only in not knowing where to stop. The result was that the Dean arrived without any difficulty, and far more quickly than I had hoped, at that point at which the truth that there is in wine unlocked his tongue to speak of the clear vision that the Tokay gave him once more. No chemist conducting experiments in his laboratory is likely to have mixed his ingredients with more care than I poured out the Tokay from now on. I mean, of course, for the Dean. I knew now how very narrow was the ridge on which his intellect perched to peer into the past; and I tended his glass with Tokay with the utmost care.

'We were talking, last time, about bones,' I said.

And if it had turned out to be the wrong thing to say I should have turned the discussion aside on to grilled bones. But no, there was nothing wrong with it. I had got him back to just the very point at which we left off last time.

'Ah, bones,' said the Dean. 'One should always bury them. Then they are there when you want them. It is something to know that, behind all the noise and panting that you may make, there is a good solid store of bones, perhaps with a bit of meat on them, put away where others can't find it. That is always a satisfaction. And then, however hungry one may feel, one knows that the meat is improving all the time. Meat has no taste until it has been hidden away awhile. It is always best to bury it. Very often, when I had nothing special to do, I would tear up a hole in the ground. I will tell you why I did that: it attracted attention. Then, if eavesdropping suspicious busybodies wanted to get your bone, they probably looked in the wrong place. It is all part of the scheme of a well-planned life: those that do not take these little precautions seldom get bones. Perhaps they may pick up a dry one now and again, but that is about all. Yes, always bury your bone.'

I noticed the dawn of what seemed a faint surprise in his face, as though something in his own words had struck him as strange, and I hastily filled his glass and placed it near his hand, which throughout the talks that I had with him had a certain wandering tendency, reminiscent to me of a butterfly in a garden; it hovered now over that golden wine, then lifted the glass, and at once he was back where his own words seemed perfectly natural to him, as indeed they did to me, for I knew that he drew them straight from the well of truth, that well whose buckets are so often delicate glasses, such as I had on my table, and which were bringing up to me now these astonishing secrets. So often I find myself referring to this Tokay, that, borrowed though it was, it may be thought I am over-proud of my cellar; but I cannot sufficiently emphasise that the whole scientific basis of my researches was the one maxim, '*in vino veritas*'; without that the Dean might have exaggerated or misinterpreted, or even have invented the whole of his story. What the law of gravity is to astronomical study, so is this Latin maxim to those investigations that I offer now to the public.

'Yes, bury your bone,' said the Dean. 'The earth is often flavourless; yet, if you choose with discrimination, in farms, beside roads, or in gardens, you hit on a delightful variety of flavours, that greatly add to your bone. I remember a favourite place of mine, just at the edge of a pig-sty, which well bore out my contention that, by a careful choice of earth, there is hardly any limit to the flavouring that may improve a buried bone or a bit of meat. For pigs themselves I have nothing at all but contempt. Their claim to be one of us is grossly exaggerated. Always chase them. Chase cows too; not that I have anything particular against them: my only reason for giving you this advice is that by this means you have their horns pointing the right way. Horns are dangerous things and, unless you chase them, they are always pointing the wrong way; which, as I need hardly say, is towards you. There is very likely some scientific reason for it, but whenever you see cows they are always coming towards you; that is to say, until you chase them. Whatever the reason is, I do not think I have ever known an exception to this natural law. Horses one should chase too: I do not exactly know why, but that is the way I feel about it. I leave them alone on a road, but if I find them in a field or on paths I always chase them. It always makes a bit of a stir when horses come by; and, if you don't chase them, the idea gets about that it is they that are making the stir, and not you. That leads to conceit among horses, and all kinds of undesirable things. That's the way I feel about it. There's just one thing to remember, and that is that, unlike cows, their dangerous end is towards you when you chase them; but no one that has ever heard the jolly sound of their hooves while being really well chased will ever think twice about that. While standing still they can kick with considerable precision, but one is not there on those occasions. While galloping their kicking is often merely silly; and, besides that, one is moving so fast oneself that one can dodge them with the utmost facility. Nothing is more exhilarating than chasing a horse. Chasing anything is good as a general rule; it keeps them moving, and you don't want things hanging around, if you will excuse the modern expression.'

The phrase made me a little uneasy, but I needn't have been, for he went straight on. 'And that brings us,' said the Dean, 'to the subject of cats.

They are sometimes amusing to chase, but on the whole they are so unreliable that chasing cats can hardly be called a sport, and must be regarded merely as a duty. Their habit of going up trees is entirely contemptible. I never object to a bird going into a tree, if I happen to have chased it off the lawn, so as to keep the lawn tidy. A tree is the natural refuge of a bird. And, besides, one can always get it out of the tree by barking. But to see a four-footed animal in a tree is a sight so revolting and disgusting that I have no words in which to describe it. Many a time I have said what I thought about that, clearly and unmistakably, and yet I have never felt that I have finally dealt with the subject. One of these days perhaps my words will be attended to, and cats may leave trees for good. Till then, till then. . .'

And I took the opportunity of his hesitation to attempt to turn the talk in a direction that might be more useful to me, if ever the time should come when this that I call I, should be what Dean Spanley had evidently been once.

CHAPTER FIVE

There was a matter that seemed to me of vital importance, if one could only get it fixed so firm in the core of one's memory that it would have a chance of survival, of surviving in fact the memory itself. This was the matter of wholesome food and water. How could one be sure of obtaining it? Sitting over a tidy table, with a clean table-cloth on it, and clean knives and forks, one may have exaggerated the importance of cleanliness; though I still feel that in the case of water such exaggeration is hardly possible. And then again I exaggerated the probability of finding oneself one day in the position I contemplated. But the vividness and sheer assurance of the Dean's memories were most conducive to this. Add to that vividness and assurance a glass or two of Tokay, and I hardly know who would have held out against the belief that such a change was quite likely. And so I said to him, 'I should object, as much as anything, to drinking bad water.'

And the Dean said: 'There is no such thing as bad water. There is water with different flavours, and giving off different smells. There is interesting water and uninteresting water. But you cannot say there is bad water.'

'But if there are really great impurities in it,' I said.

'It makes it all the more interesting,' said the Dean. 'If the impurities are so thick that it is solid, then it ceases to be water. But while it is water it is always good.'

I may have looked a trifle sick; for the Dean looked up and said to me reassuringly, 'No, no, never trouble yourself about that.'

I said no more for a while: it seemed hardly worth the trouble to drive and drive into one's memory, till they became almost part of one's character, little pieces of information that might perhaps survive the great change, if the information was no better than this. Of food I had heard his views already; the whole thing seemed disgusting; but I decided that in the interests of science it was my duty to get all the facts I could from the Dean.

So I threw in a word to keep him to the subject, and sat back and listened.

'It is the same with meat,' he went on. 'When meat can no longer be eaten, it is no longer there. It disappears. Bones remain always, but meat disappears. It has a lovely smell before it goes; and then fades away like a dream.'

'I am not hungry,' I said.

And indeed truer word was never spoken, for my appetite was entirely lost. 'Shall we talk of something else for a bit? If you don't mind. What about sport? Rats, for instance.'

'Our wainscot was not well stocked with game,' said the Dean; 'either rats or mice. I have hunted rats, but not often. There is only one thing to remember at this sport: shake the rat. To shake the rat is essential. I need hardly tell you how to do that, because I think everybody is born to it. It is not merely a method of killing the rat, but it prevents him from biting you. He must be shaken until he is dead. Mice of course are small game.'

'What is the largest game you have ever hunted?' I asked. For he had stopped talking, and it was essential to the interests of these researches that he should be kept to the same mood.

'A traction-engine.' replied the Dean.

That dated him within fifty years or so; and I decided that that incarnation of his was probably some time during the reign of Queen Victoria.

'The thing came snorting along our road, and I saw at once that it had to be chased. I couldn't allow a thing of that sort on our flower-beds, and very likely coming into the house. A thing like that might have done anything, if not properly chased at once. So I ran round and chased it. It shouted and threw black stones at me. But I chased it until it was well past our gate. It was very hard to the teeth, very big, very noisy and slow. They can't turn round on you like rats. They are made for defence rather than for attack. Much smaller game is often more dangerous than traction-engines.'

So clearly did I picture the traction-engine on that Victorian road, with a dog yapping at the back wheels, that I wondered more and more what kind of a dog, in order to complete the mental picture. And that was the question I began to ask the Dean. 'What kind of a dog————?' I began. But the question was much harder to ask than it may appear. My guest looked somehow so diaconal, that the words froze on my lips; and, try as I would, I could not frame the sentence: what kind of a dog were you? It seems silly, I know, to say that it was impossible merely to say seven words; and yet I found it so. I cannot explain it. I can only suggest to any that cannot credit this incapacity, that they should address those words themselves to any senior dignitary of the church, and see whether they do not themselves feel any slight hesitancy. I turned my question aside, and only lamely asked, 'What kind of a dog used they to keep?'

He asked me who I meant. And I answered: 'The people that you were talking about.'

Thus sometimes conversations dwindle to trivial ends.

Many minutes passed before I gathered again the lost threads of that conversation. For nearly ten minutes I dared hardly speak, so near he seemed to the light of to-day, so ready to turn away from the shadows he saw so clearly, moving in past years. I poured out for him more Tokay, and he absently drank it, and only gradually returned to that reminiscent mood that had been so gravely disturbed by the clumsiness of my question. Had I asked the Dean straight out, 'What kind of a dog were you?' I believe he would have answered satisfactorily. But the very hesitancy of my question had awakened suspicion at once, as though the question had been a guilty thing. I was not sure that he was safely back in the past again until he made a petulant remark about another engine, a remark so obviously untrue that it may not seem worth recording; I only repeat it here as it showed that the Dean had returned to his outlook over the reaches of time, and that he seems to have been contemporary with the threshing-machine. 'Traction-engines!' he said with evident loathing. 'I saw one scratching itself at the back of a haystack. I thoroughly barked at it.'

'They should be barked at,' I said, as politely as I could.

'Most certainly,' said the Dean. 'If things like that got to think they could go where they liked without any kind of protest, we should very soon have them everywhere.'

And there was so much truth in that that I was able to agree with the Dean in all sincerity.

'And then where should we all be?' the Dean asked.

And that is a question unfortunately so vital to all of us, that I think it is sufficient to show by itself that the Dean was not merely wandering. It seemed to me that the bright mind of a dog had seen, perhaps in the seventies of the last century, a menace to which the bulk of men must have been blind; or we should never be over-run by machines as we are, in every sense of the word. He was talking sense here. Was it not therefore fair to suppose he was speaking the truth, even where his words were surprising? If I had faintly felt that I was doing something a little undignified in lowering myself to the level of what, for the greater part of these conversations, was practically the mind of a dog, I no longer had that feeling after this observation the Dean had uttered about machinery. Henceforth I felt that he was at least my equal; even when turning, as he soon did, from philosophical speculation, he returned to talk of the chase.

'To chase anything slow,' he said, 'is always wearisome. You are continually bumping into what you are chasing. There is nothing so good as a ball. A ball goes so fast that it draws out your utmost speed, in a very exhilarating manner, and it can jump about as far as one can oneself, and before one can begin to be tired, it always slows down. And then it takes a long time to eat; so that, one way and another, there is more entertainment in a ball than perhaps anything else one can chase. If one could throw it oneself, like the Masters, I cannot imagine any completer life than throwing a ball and chasing it all day long.'

My aim was purely scientific; I desired to reveal to Europeans a lore taught throughout Asia, but neglected, so far as I knew, by all our investigators; I desired to serve science only. Had it been otherwise, the momentary temptation that came to me as the Dean spoke now might possibly have prevailed; I might possibly have hurried on some slight excuse from the room and come back with an old tennis-ball, and perhaps have suddenly thrown it, and so have gratified that sense of the ridiculous that is unfortunately in all of us, at the expense of more solid study.

CHAPTER SIX

The temptation to which I referred in the last
chapter was far too trivial a thing to have its place
in this record, or indeed in any summary of investigations that may claim to be of value to science.
It should certainly have never arisen. And yet,
having arisen, it enforces its place amongst my
notes; for, my researches being of necessity conversational, whatever turned the current of the conversation between the Dean and myself becomes of
scientific importance. And that this unfortunately
frivolous fancy, that came so inopportunely, did
actually affect the current of our conversation is
regrettably only too true. For about five minutes I
was unable to shake it off, and during all that time,
knowing well how inexcusable such action would
be, I dared scarcely move or speak. Dean Spanley
therefore continued his reminiscences unguided

by me, and sometimes wandered quite away from the subject. I might indeed have lost him altogether; I mean to say, as a scientific collaborator; for during that five minutes I never even filled his glass. Luckily I pulled myself together in time, banished from my mind entirely that foolish and trivial fancy, and resumed the serious thread of my researches by saying to the Dean: 'What about ticks?'

'It is not for us to deal with them.' said the Dean. 'The Wise Ones, the Masters, can get them out. Nobody else can. It is of no use therefore to scratch. One's best policy towards a tick is summed up in the words, "Live and let live." That is to say, when the tick has once taken up his abode. When the tick is still wild it is a good thing to avoid him, by keeping away from the grasses in which they live, mostly in marshy places, unless led there by anything exciting, in which case it is of course impossible to think of ticks.'

This fatalistic attitude to a tick, when once it had burrowed in, so strangely different from the view that we take ourselves, did as much as anything else in these strange experiences to decide me that the Dean was actually remembering clearly where the rest of us forget almost totally; standing, as it were, a solitary traveller near one bank of the river of Lethe, and hearing his memories calling shrill through the mist that conceals the opposite shore. From now on I must say that I considered the whole thing proved, and only concerned myself to gather as many facts as possible for the benefit of science, a benefit that I considered it only fair that I should share myself, to the extent of obtaining any useful hints that I could for use in any other sojourn, in the event of my ever meeting with an experience similar to Dean Spanley's and being able to preserve the memory of what I had learned from him. Now that I considered his former sojourn proved (though of course I do not claim to be the sole judge of that) I questioned Dean Spanley about what seems to many of us one of the most mysterious things in the animal world, the matter of scent. To the Dean there seemed nothing odd in it, and I suppose the mystery lies largely in the comparative weakness of that sense among us.

'How long would you be able to follow a man.' I said, 'after he had gone by?'

'That depends on the weather,' said the Dean. 'Scent is never the same two days running. One might be able to follow after he had gone half an hour. But there is one thing that one should bear in mind, and that is that, if any of the Masters in their superb generosity should chance to give one cheese, one cannot, for some while after that, follow with any certainty. The question of scent is of course a very subtle one, and cannot be settled lightly. The view that the Archbishop takes, er, er, is. . .'

The moment had come for which I had been watching all the evening, the moment when the Dean was waking up from the dream, or falling asleep from the reality, whichever way one should put it, the moment at which any words of his own describing his other sojourn would, upon pene-trating those diaconal ears, cause the most painful surprise. Twice before it had happened; and I felt that if it happened again I might no more be able to get the Dean to dine with me. Science might go no further in this direction, in Europe. So I said, 'Excuse me a moment. The telephone, I think.' And rushed out of the room.

When I came back our conversation was not, I trust, without interest; but as it was solely con-cerned with the new lift that it is proposed to install in the club to which Dean Spanley and I belong, not many of my readers would easily follow

the plans, were I to describe them here, or understand the importance of the new lift.

I pass over the next few weeks. The Dean dined
with me once more, but I was not able to persuade
him to take sufficient Tokay to enable him to have
that wonderful view of his that looked back down
the ages, or indeed to see anything of any interest
at all. He talked to me, but told me nothing that
any reasonably well-educated reader could not
find out for himself in almost any library. He was
far far short of the point to which I had hoped my
Tokay would bring him. I felt a renegade to science. There are those who will understand my difficulties; he was naturally an abstemious man; he
was a dean; and he was by now entirely familiar
with the exact strength of Tokay; it was not so easy
to persuade him by any means whatever to go so
far with that wine as he had gone three times
already, three lapses that he must have at least suspected, if he did not even know exactly all about
them. There are those who will understand all this.
But there are others who in view of what was at
stake will be absolutely ruthless; scientists who, in
the study of some new or rare disease, would not
hesitate to inoculate themselves with it, were it necessary to study it so, men who would never spare

themselves while working for Science, and who will not withhold criticism from me. What prevented me, they will ask, from forcing upon Dean Spanley, by any means whatever, sufficient alcohol for these important researches? For such a revelation as was awaiting a few more glasses of wine, any means would have been justified.

It is easy to argue thus. But a broader mind will appreciate that you cannot ask a man to dine with you, let alone a dean, and then by trickery or violence, or whatever it is that some may lightly recommend, reduce him to a state that is far beyond any that he would willingly cultivate. All the permissible arts of a host I had already exercised. Beyond that I would not go. Meanwhile what was I to do? I felt like Keats' watcher of the skies when some new planet swims into his ken, and when almost immediately afterwards some trivial obstacle intervenes; a blind is drawn down, a fog comes up, or perhaps a small cloud; and the wonder one knows to be there is invisible. Much I had learned already, and I trust that what I have written has scientific value, but I wanted the whole story. I was no more content than a man would be who had obtained twenty or thirty pages of an ancient codex, if he knew that there were hundreds of pages of it. And what I sought seemed so near, and yet out of my grasp, removed from me by perhaps two small glasses. I never lost my temper with the Dean, and when I found that I could no more question him stimulated, I questioned him sober. This was perhaps the most enraging experience of all; for not only was Dean Spanley extremely reticent, but he did not really know anything. An intense understanding of dogs, a sympathy for their more reputable emotions, and a guess that a strange truth may have been revealed to Hindus, was about all he had to tell. I have said already that I knew he had a secret; and this knowledge was what started me on my researches; but this secret of his amounted to no more knowledge, as a scientist uses the word, than a few exotic shells bought in some old shop, on a trip to the seaside can supply a knowledge of seafaring. Between the Dean sober at the Olympus Club, and the same Dean after his fourth glass of Tokay, was all the difference between some such tripper as I have indicated, and a wanderer familiar with the surf of the boundaries of the very farthest seas. It was annoying, but it was so. And then it seemed to me that perhaps where I had just failed alone I might be able to succeed with the help of example, if I asked one or two others to meet the Dean. I was thinking in the form of a metaphor particularly unsuited to Tokay, 'You may lead a horse to water, but you cannot make him drink.' And from thinking of horses I got the idea of a lead out hunting, and so the idea of a little company at dinner easily came to me, one or two of the right kind who could be trusted to give a lead.

And I found the very man. And the moment I found him I decided that no more were necessary; just he and I and the Dean would make a perfect dinner-party, from which I hoped that so much was to be revealed. I found him sitting next to me at a public dinner, a man of the most charming address, and with an appreciation of good wine that was evidently the foremost of all his accomplishments. He was so much a contrast to the man on the other side of me, that I turned to Wrather (that was his name) quite early in the dinner and talked to him for the rest of the evening. The man on the other side of me was not only a teetotaller, which anybody may be, but one that wanted to convert his neighbours; and he started on me as soon as the sherry came round, so that it was a pleasure to hear from Wrather what was almost his first remark to me: 'Never trust a teetotaller, or a man that wears elastic-sided boots.' The idea struck me at once that he might be the man I wanted; and when I saw how well he was guided by the spirit of that saying, both in dress and in habits, I decided that he actually was. Later in that evening he put an arm round my shoulders and said:

'You're younger than me; not with the whole of your life before you, but some of it; and this advice may be useful to you: Never trust a teetotaller, or a man that wears elastic-sided boots.'

One doesn't see elastic-sided boots as much now as one used to, and I fancied that he had evolved his saying early in life, or that perhaps it was handed down to him.

We made great friends, and as we went out from the dinner together I tried to help him into his coat. He could not find the arm-hole, and said, 'Never mind. I shall never find it. Throw the damned thing over my shoulders.'

Which I did. And he added, 'But for all that, never trust a teetotaller, or a man that wears elastic-sided boots.'

We shared a taxi and, in the darkness of it, he talked as delightfully as he had in the bright hall where we had dined; until, suddenly seeing a policeman, he stopped the cab and leaned out and shouted, 'Bobby! There's something I want to tell you; and it's worth all you've ever learnt in Scotland Yard.'

The constable came up slowly.

'Look here,' said Wrather. 'It's this. Never trust a teetotaller, or a man that wears elastic-sided boots.'

'We've been dining with the Woolgatherers,' I said through a chink beside Wrather.

And the constable nodded his head and walked slowly away.

'Sort of thing that will set him up,' said Wrather; 'if only he can remember it.'

CHAPTER SEVEN

I called on Wrather the very next day and told him
about the dinner with the Dean. I did not talk science or philosophy with Wrather, because he was
not interested in science, and as far as I could
gather from the talk of a single evening the tenets
of transmigration did not appeal to him. But I told
him that the Dean kept a dog, and knew a great
deal about dogs, and that when he had had a few
glasses he thought he *was* a dog, and told dog-
stories that were amusing and instructive. I told
Wrather straight out that the Dean went very slow
with wine, and that to get any amusement out of
him he must be encouraged to take his whack like
a reasonable sportsman. Wrather said very little,
but there was a twinkle in his eye, that showed me I
could rely on him whenever I should be able to get
the Dean. And I think that there may have been

also in Wrather's mind, like a dim memory, the idea that I had helped him with a policeman, and he felt grateful. I watched next for the Dean at the club, and soon found him, and said that I hoped he would dine with me one day again, as I particularly wanted to ask him about the Greek strategy at Troy, a subject that I had found out he was keen on. He may have been a little afraid of that Tokay; on the other hand it attracted him. A man of the Dean's degree of refinement could hardly fail to have been attracted by the Tokay, if he knew anything about wine at all; and Dean Spanley certainly did. He was not unpleased to be consulted by me about the Greek strategy; no man is entirely unmoved by being asked for information upon his particular subject; and he was very anxious to tell me about it. The final touch that may have decided him to accept my invitation was that he had beaten my Tokay last time, and so may well have thought that his fear of it was ungrounded. But an estimate of the Dean's motives in accepting my invitation to dinner may not be without an element of specula- tion; the bare fact remains that he did accept it. It was to be for the Wednesday of the following week, and I hurried round to Wrather again and got him to promise to come on that day. I told him now still more about the Dean: I said that I was a writer, and wanted to get some of the Dean's stories; but there are many different kinds of writers, and I was far from telling Wrather what kind I was, for I knew that, had I told him I was a scientist, I should merely have bored him; I let him therefore suppose that I wanted the Dean's dog-stories only for what might be humorous in them, and he never at any time had an inkling of the value of what I sought, the Golconda of knowledge that was lying so close to me. I told him that Tokay was the key to what I was after, and that the Dean was rather difficult. 'Did I ever tell you,' asked Wrather, 'a maxim that my old father taught me? Never trust a teetotaller, or a man who wears elastic-sided boots.'

'Yes, I think you did,' I answered. 'But Dean Spanley is not a teetotaller. Only goes a bit slow, you know.'

'We'll shove him along,' said Wrather.

And I saw from a look in his eye that Wrather would do his best.

And certainly Wrather did do his best when the night came. To begin with he appreciated the Tokay for its own sake. But there was a certain whimsical charm about him that almost compelled you to take a glass with him when he urged you to do so in the way that he had. I know that what I am telling you is very silly. Why should a man take a glass of wine for himself because another man is taking one for him self? And yet it is one of those ways of the world that I have not been able to check. Some abler man than I may one day alter it. We did not come to the Tokay at once; we began on champagne. And certainly Dean Spanley went very slow with it, as I saw from a certain humorous and mournful look on the face of Wrather, as much as I did by watching the glass of the Dean. And in the end we came to the Tokay; and Wrather goaded the Dean to it.

'I don't suppose that a dean drinks Tokay,' said Wrather, gazing thoughtfully at his own glass.

'And why not?' asked the Dean.

'They are so sure of Heaven hereafter,' said Wrather, 'that they don't have to grab a little of it wherever they can, like us poor devils.'

'Ahem,' said the Dean, and looked at the glass that I had poured out for him, the merits of which he knew just as well as Wrather.

'And then they're probably afraid of doing anything that people like me do, thinking we're all bound for Hell, and that their names might get mixed up by mistake with ours at the Day of Judgment, if they kept company with us too much.'

'Oh, I wouldn't say that,' said the Dean.

I tried to stop Wrather after a while, thinking he went too far; but he wouldn't leave Dean Spanley alone: I had set Wrather on to him, and now I found that I could not call him off. At any rate the Dean drank his Tokay. 'Well, what more do you want?' Wrather seemed to say to me with a single glance of his expressive eyes, knowing perfectly well that I was trying to stop him. It was then that I asked the Dean about the Greek strategy at Troy. Dean Spanley put down his third glass of Tokay and began to tell me about it, and a look came over Wrather's face that was altogether pro-Trojan, or at any rate against everything to do with the Greeks. As the Dean talked on I poured out another glass of Tokay for him and watched him, and Wrather watched too. He was getting near to that point at which the curious change took place: I knew that by little signs that I had noted before. Wrather sat now quite silent, seeming to know as much as I did of the effect of the Tokay on the Dean, though he had not ever seen him drink it before. But he was not there yet. I need not say what a thousand writers have said, that alcohol dulls the memory; I need not say what has been said for three thousand years, that wine sharpens the wit; both of these things are true; and both were to be observed in the same Dean. Some minds are more easily affected than others: when forgetfulness came to the Dean it came suddenly and very completely; had it not done so he would never have spoken out as he did. And right on top of the forgetfulness came this other phenomenon, the intense brightening of another part of the mind, a part of the mind that others of us may not possess, but far more likely, I think, a part that in most of us has never happened to be illuminated. It was, as I have said before, on only a narrow ridge that this occurred even with the Dean, only for a short while, only after that precise glass, that exact number of drops of Tokay, that makes the rest of us think, upon careful reflection long after, that we may have perhaps taken a drop more than was strictly advisable. This ridge, this moment, this drop, was now approaching the Dean, and Wrather and I sat watching.

'If we compare the siege of Troy with more modern sieges,' said the Dean, 'or the siege of Ilion, as I prefer to call it, one finds among obvious differences a similarity of general principle.'

Only he did not say the word principle; his tongue bungled it, went back and tried it again, tripped over it and fell downstairs. An effort that he made to retrieve the situation showed me the moment had come.

'Good dog,' I said.

A momentary surprise flickered on Wrather's face, but with the Dean bright memory shone on the heels of forgetfulness. 'Eh?' he said. 'Wag was my name. Though not my only one. On rare occasions, very precious to me, I have been called "Little Devil".'

The surprise cleared from Wrather's face, and a look of mild interest succeeded it, as when a connoisseur notes a new manifestation.

Any difficulty the Dean had had with his tongue had entirely disappeared.

'Ah, those days,' he said. 'I used to spend a whole morning at it.'

'At what?' I asked.

'At hunting,' said the Dean, as though that should have been understood. 'Ah, I can taste to this day, all the various tastes of digging out a rabbit. How fresh they were.'

'What tastes?' I asked. For however tedious exactitude may be to some, it is bread and jam to a scientist.

'The brown earth,' he said. 'And sometimes chalk when one got down deeper, a totally different taste, not so pleasant, not quite so meaty. And then the sharp taste of the juicy roots of trees, that almost always have to be bitten in two while digging out a rabbit. And little unexpected tastes; dead leaves, and even a slug. They are innumerable, and all delightful. And all the while, you know, there is that full ample scent of the rabbit, growing deeper and deeper as you get farther in, till it is almost food to breathe it. The scent grows deeper, the air grows warmer, the home of the rabbit grows darker, and his feet when he moves sound like thunder; and all the while one's own magnificent scratchings sweep towards him. Winds blowing in past one's shoulders with scents from outside are forgotten. And at the end of it all is one's rabbit. That is indeed a moment.'

'Some dean,' muttered Wrather. An interruption such as no student of science would welcome at such a time. But I forgave him, for he had served science already far better than he could know, and I hushed him with a look, and the Dean went on.

'It may be,' said the Dean, 'though I cannot analyse it, but it may be that the actual eating of one's rabbit is no more thrilling than that gradual approach as one gnaws one's way through the earth. What would you say?'

'I should say it was equal,' I answered.

'And you, Mr Wrather?' said the Dean.

'Not very good at definitions, you know,' said Wrather. 'But I will say one thing: one should never trust a teetotaller, or a man that wears elastic-sided boots.'

And I could see that he was warming towards the Dean; so that, trivial though such a thought is for a scientist to entertain in the middle of such researches, I saw that my little dinner-party would at any rate go well, as the saying is.

'There is one thing to bear in mind on those occasions,' said the Dean, fingering his collar with a touch of uneasiness, 'and that is getting back again. When one's dinner is over one wants to get back. And if the root of a tree, that one has per-haps bitten through, or a thin flint pointing the wrong way, should get under one's collar, it may produce a very difficult situation.'

His face reddened a little over his wide white collar even at the thought. And it is not a situation to laugh at.

'Where your head and shoulders have gone they can get back again,' the Dean continued; 'were it not for the collar. That is the danger. One does not think of that while eating one's rabbit, but it is always a risk, especially where there are roots of trees. There have been cases in which that very thing has happened; caught by the collar. I knew of a case myself. Someone was lost, and men were looking for him in our woods. Of course they could not smell. But I happened to be out for a walk, and I noticed a trail leading straight to a rabbit-hole, a very old trail indeed, but when one put one's nose to the hole the dog was undoubtedly down there, and had been there a long time. He must have been caught. I expect by the collar.'

'And what did you do for him?' I couldn't help blurting out.

'He was nobody I knew,' said the Dean.

CHAPTER EIGHT

Wrather turned his face slowly round and looked at me; and I could see that the feeling of friendship that he had had for the Dean when he found he was not a teetotaller had suddenly all veered away. For myself I cared nothing for the Dean, one way or the other, except as the only link that Europe is known to have between the twentieth century and lives that roamed other ages. As such he was of inestimable value, so that the callousness that was so repulsive to Wrather had no more effect upon me than a distorted bone has on a surgeon; it was just one manifestation of a strange case.

'Are you sure he hasn't elastic-sided boots?' murmured Wrather to me. An absurd question about any member of the Olympus Club. And I treated it with silence accordingly. And out of that silence arose Dean Spanley's voice, with a touch of the monotony that is sometimes heard in the voice of a man who is deep in reminiscence, far away from those he addresses.

'It's a grand life, a dog's life,' he said.

'If one thinks one's a dog,' muttered Wrather to me, 'one should think one is a decent kind of a dog.'

Dean Spanley never heard him, and rambled on: 'It is undoubtedly the most perfect form of enjoyment that can be known. Where else shall we find those hourly opportunities for sport, romance and adventure, combined with a place on the rugs of the wisest and greatest? And then the boundless facilities for an ample social life. One has only to sniff at the wheel of a cart to have news of what is going on, sometimes as much as five miles away. I remember once sniffing at a wheel myself, and I found that there was a fellow who had been doing the same at a distance of nearly ten miles. And in the end I got to know him. He came one day with the cart, and I recognised him at once. We had a bit of a fight at first; on my part because I had to show him that the house was properly guarded and that it could not allow strangers, and he in order to show that that wheel was his. We fought on a patch of grass that there was near the back door. There was a grip that I used to be fond of; the ear. The throat-grip is of course final, but as nobody ever lets you in at it, or hardly ever, I used to think that it was waste of time to try for it, and I concentrated upon an ear. The ear was my speciality. Well, I got him by one of the ears and he shouted: "I am a poor dog! I am being most dreadfully maltreated ! I am far away from home and I am being killed in a cruel country! I am the favourite dog of very great and magnificent people! They would weep to see me killed like this. They brought me up very nicely! I am a poor dog! Oh! Oh! Oh! All is over with me now! It is the end! I was a poor good dog. But now I am quite dead." I remember his words to this day. And then a lady came out from the kitchen with a bucket; and she had always a very high opinion of me, a very high opinion indeed, and treated me with the utmost consideration; but to-day she must have had some disappointment, for she acted with the bucket in a way quite unlike herself. Indeed I will not even say what she did with the bucket. It was a hasty act, and quite spoiled the fight. She did it without reflection.

'The other fellow licked the side of his paw and smoothed down his ear with it. "Very powerful and angry people you have here," he said.

'"Not at all," I said. "She's never like that as a rule. She must have had some disappointment."

'"Never mind," he said, "it was a good fight, as far as it went."

'"But I can't understand her spoiling it," I said. "I don't know what disappointed her."

'"Oh, they're the same everywhere," he said. "I have seen people act just as hastily with a broom."

'We sat and talked like that: how clearly it all comes back to me. And from that we came to talking about sport. And I said that our woods held a lot of very big game. And we arranged a little party of him and me, and set out to hunt the woods there and then. And the very first thing we came to was a great big smell of an enormous animal, and a great enemy of Man, and much too near the house, a fox. And we sat down and said should we hunt him? He was somewhere quite close, the smell was lying on the ground in great heaps and stretched as high up as you could jump. And we sat and thought for a while as to whether we ought to hunt him. And in the end the other fellow decided. I remember his words to this day. "Perhaps not," he said. So we went on then after rabbits. The woods were on a slope, and near the top there were brambles. I put him into the brambles and ran along the outside a little ahead of him at the edge of the trees. There were rabbits in those brambles that didn't properly belong to our wood at all: they came in there from the open land, to keep warm. So when my friend put one out, he ran to the open country that he had come from, over the top of the hill; and I gave a shout or two and we both went after him, and it was just the country for a hunt, no bushes or brambles where the rabbit could play tricks, good short grass very nice for the feet, and fine air for shouting in.

'The rabbit, as you know, has been given a white tail to guide us, so that we did not need to take any trouble to keep him in sight. He went over the top of the hill, smooth grass all the way, with nothing else but a few ant-heaps, and down the side of a valley: his home was a long way off, and it would have been a lovely hunt had he not resorted to trickery. We came to a thick hedge, full of trees, and he went in and hopped about the thorns and round the trunks of trees in a silly sort of way, and in and out among brambles; in fact the whole thing got so stupid that after a while we decided to have no more to do with the silly thing. I said, "Let's hunt something more sensible."

'And he said, "Let's."

'I don't waste my time on folk that fool about among brambles. Well, we got back to the wood, and we went along taking observations in the air. Winds, you know, blew down paths and between trees, and we noted what was at the other end of the wind. And we hadn't gone far when there was a very strange scent indeed, quite close, and there was a big hole in the chalk and the scent coming pouring out of it. "You have big game in your woods," said my friend.

'"Very big game indeed," I said.

'And we went up to the hole. There was a badger at home down there, and he seemed to be asleep. So we decided to wake him up. We just put our mouths right into the hole and barked at him. He was a long way down, but he must have heard us. We barked at him for ten minutes. It was the greatest fun. Then we went on through the wood, and presently what should we see but a very showy young rabbit who was out on a long walk, no doubt for social reasons. So we chased the young fellow all through the wood and back to his own house. It was a very populous neighbourhood, and we didn't stop and dig; too many passages, you know, running in all directions. So I said: "Let's come and hunt a large bad animal."

'It was a pig that I meant, but that's how one puts it. You know the sniff beside the other fellow's face, and the beckoning of the head, that means that?'

I merely nodded: I was not going to interrupt the Dean just now with a request for explanations. And I looked at Wrather, in case he was going to do so; but Wrather sat silent and interested.

'He said, "Let's." And I said, "I know where there is one." And I ran on in front.

'So we came to the pig's house and looked in through his door at him and shouted, "Pig." He didn't like that. He looked just like a pig; he was a pig; and he knew it. He came towards his door saying silly surly things in a deep voice. You know the kind of talk. And we just shouted, "Pig. Pig. Pig." Both of us, for nearly half an hour. It was perfectly splendid and we enjoyed it immensely.'

'What did he say?' asked Wrather.

'What could he say?' said the Dean. 'He knew he was a pig. But he didn't like being told about it. I've seldom enjoyed myself more. It made up for that fool of a rabbit that was so silly in the hedge on the hill.

'Then we went to the back of the stables and rolled in something nice, till our coats were

smooth and we both had a beautiful scent. Then
we killed a hen for the fun of it. It was a lovely
evening.

'It was getting all dark and late now. In fact, if I
stayed any longer, there would be terrible beatings.
So I said: "What about your cart?" And he said: 'It
has a long way to go. I can catch that up when I
like. We live three overs away."'

'Overs?' I said.

'Dips over the hills,' said the Dean.

And I did not like to question him further, for
fear that it would bring him back to our own day.
But what I think he meant was a distance of three
horizons.

'I said, "Very well, old fellow, then we'll have a
bit more sport."

'"What shall it be?" he said.

'And even as he spoke a thing I had been sus-
pecting happened on top of the hill. There'd been
a suspicious light there for some time; not the
right kind of light; a touch too much of magic in it
to my liking; a thing to be watched. And sure
enough the moon rose. It was of course my job to
guard the house when the moon came large and
sudden over that hill, as I have known it do before,
but now that I had my friend with me I said, "Shall

we hunt it?" And he said, "Oh, let's." And we went up that hill quicker than we went after the rabbit; and when we got to the top we barked at the moon. And lucky for the moon he didn't stay where he was. And the longer we stayed the stranger the shadows got. Soon it was magic all round us, and more than one dog could bark at. Very magic indeed.

'When we had hunted the moon enough we came back through the wood; and we both of us growled as we came to the trees, so as to warn whatever there was in the darkness, in case it should try to threaten us. There were lots of things in the wood that were hand-in-glove with the moon, queer things that did not bark or move or smell, and one could not see them, but one knew they were there. We came back down the hill with our mouths wide open, so as to breathe in all the pleasantness of that day: we had hunted a badger, two rabbits, a hen, a pig and the moon, and very nearly a fox; and I had a feeling I have not often had, that it was almost enough. And my friend said, "I must go after my cart now, or the man will be thinking he's lost." And I said "Let me know how you are, next time your cart is coming this way." And he promised he would. And I promised to let him know how I was, whenever the cart came.'

'He thinks he is one, all right,' said Wrather to me.

'I beg your pardon?' said the Dean.

'Nothing,' said Wrather. 'Something we were talking about the other day. I've let the Tokay stop in front of me. I *beg* your pardon.' And he passed it on to the Dean. We watched Dean Spanley, thus encouraged, pour out another glass. He drank a little, and Wrather continued, 'But you were telling me about a very interesting evening.'

'Yes, it was interesting,' said the Dean. 'I remember coming back to the house, and it was late and the door was unfortunately shut. And I knocked, but nobody came to it. And I had to shout, "I am out in the cold." "I am out in the cold," I shouted; "and the moon is after me. It is a terrible night and I shall die in the cold, and my ghost will haunt this house. My ghost will wail in the house when the cold and the moon have killed me. I am a poor dog out in the dark."

'Those were my very words; it made me very sad to hear myself saying them, and my tail drooped under me and my voice became very mournful. Then they came and opened the door; the Wise Ones, the Great Ones. And then they beat me with a stick. And of course I said, "I am only a poor dog;

~ 79 ~

a poor destitute dog overcome with profound shame, who will never sin again." And, when the beating stopped, everything was very very beautiful.

'I went into the kitchen then and said to them there: "I have had a splendid beating, and I am not at all the dog that I was before, but am utterly purged of sin, and I am wise now and good and never shall sin again, but I am very hungry." I am telling you the exact words that I used, because they happen to be very clear in my memory. I don't know if my reminiscences interest you.'

'Profoundly,' said Wrather. 'But I hope you aren't expecting me to drink all the Tokay by myself, and then perhaps going to laugh at me afterwards.'

'Not at all,' said the Dean.

And he took a little more, though not much, and went on with his reminiscences, while I applauded Wrather as far as one can by a look. 'They gave me a very beautiful dinner. They were good women of great wisdom. And when I had fin-ished what they had given me, and I had cleaned the plate as one should, I was fortunate enough to find a good deal of bacon-rind, which was kept in a treasury that I knew of, and which by a great piece of luck was well mixed with some jam and some pieces of cheese, and a good deal of broom-sweepings, with several different flavours, and one sausage, which happened to be old enough to give a distinct taste to the whole dish. It was a lovely dinner; and I knew that the moon would not dare to come back again after all I and the other fellow had said to him, so there was really no more to be done when they took me to bed. And I walked round eight or nine times on the straw, till my bed was just right, and I lay down and the night went away, and all the world was awake again.'

CHAPTER NINE

'When all the world woke up,' the Dean went rambling on, 'there were the voices of a great many things that had come too close, impudent folk like birds, that had to be chased. So I shouted, asking to be let out at once. For a long while no one came, and then I heard a voice saying something about all this noise, which was just what I had been calling his attention to; and he let me out, but I think he had been worried overnight by the moon or one of those prowling things, for he did not look glad. And I ran out and chased everything that needed chasing. And so another day started.'

'You must have been the hell of a dog,' said Wrather suddenly.

That spoiled everything. To begin with, talk of any sort was rather liable to bring him back to the present day; and, besides that, it was not the way to address a dean. That he had once used similar words himself did not excuse Wrather. In any case Dean Spanley, so far as I had observed him, never stayed for very long with his mind's eye open upon that strange past and shut to this age of ours. He started slightly now, and I indicated the bottle of Tokay, nearly empty, and then glanced towards Wrather, to account for, if not to excuse, the unfortunate words.

'When I was up at Oxford,' said the Dean, 'I was certainly a young man of some, shall I say, considerable activity. But a dog in any sense of the word, let alone one qualified by the word you used, would be a much exaggerated way of describing me.'

'Certainly. Quite so,' I said.

And the incident passed off, while we both turned somewhat pitying eyes upon Wrather.

'You know, you're a bit overcome,' I said to Wrather.

And Wrather understood me.

'I expect that's it,' he said. And he took the line that I indicated.

It is curious that, of all the amazing things said in that room, the words that made far the most stir was the almost innocent remark of Wrather. And I am sure that Dean Spanley believed that this remark was the strangest that had been made there that evening. This was as it should be; but, while it left the way open for another dinner, it certainly made it difficult to get the Dean to meet Wrather.

Our little dinner-party soon broke up; the Dean was a trifle shocked at Wrather's lapse with the Tokay; Wrather was a bit ashamed of himself for having spoiled the sport, as he put it afterwards; and I had no longer any scientific interest in the dinner, as I realised that the Dean would not go back through the years any more that night. I merely remained an ordinary host. I do not think it was any hardship on Wrather to have been suspected of drunkenness, for he had brought it all on himself; incidentally he had had an enormous amount of Tokay, but only incidentally, for it had no real effect on Wrather. We all went downstairs, and I called a taxi, into which I put the Dean. Then Wrather came back into the house with me. Going upstairs he apologised for having 'undogged the Dean,' and then we came to a room in which I sit and smoke a good deal, and we sat in front of the fire in armchairs and talked of Dean Spanley. And Wrather, with the air of a man who has been slightly cheated, said: 'Have you noticed that he told us nothing of any love-affair?'

'No,' I said. 'He didn't. I wonder why.'

'Too much dean still left in him,' said Wrather. 'You must get him deeper.'

'Deeper?' I said.

'More Tokay,' said Wrather.

It was all very well for Wrather to say that, but it couldn't be done. Besides which, I was by no means certain how wide that ridge was from which the Dean saw the past: at a certain number of glasses he arrived there; might not two extra glasses topple him down beyond it, and, if so, where? Then Wrather, though he had no idea how much was at stake scientifically, was distinctly helpful. 'I think he is there all the time; in his dog-kennel, you know,' he said. 'Only, in the glare of to-day, he can't see it. That Tokay of yours is just like pulling down a blind on the glare, and then the old dog can see. Keep him full of it and you should have some sport with him.'

The flippancy of these remarks is obvious. But I give them to my reader for the element of truth that I think they contained, for flashes of truth may often appear to an insight even as unscientific as Wrather's. Moreover Wrather's view bore out the idea that I had long ago formed, that Dean Spanley in broad daylight at his club knew something veiled from the rest of us, though too little to be of any real value, until he was entirely removed from unfavourable conditions. And this removal my Tokay seemed to accomplish.

'It's all very well,' I said rather crossly, 'for you to say keep him full of Tokay. But he won't drink it for me, not to any extent. He would for you somehow; but you've spoilt it all by calling him a dog, which is a thing no dean would stand.'

'I'm sorry,' said Wrather. 'Let's think what we can do. You know I'm as keen as you are to hear the old dog talk.'

That this was not the way to speak of Dean Spanley will be clear to my readers, but I said nothing of that then, and, instead of touching on any such delicate matter, we hatched a somewhat childish plot between us.

The plot went like this, and it was mainly Wrather's idea: the Dean would not want to meet a drunken fellow like Wrather again; no dignitary of the church, no member of an important club, would. But represent Wrather as a man needing guidance, represent him as something much worse than what he had appeared to Dean Spanley, or anything he had ever been, a man about to be wrecked on the rocks of Tokay (if a liquid may be compared to a rock), and Wrather argued and I came to agree, and we hatched the thing out together, the Dean would come to save an almost hopeless case; and, if he got a few glasses of the finest Tokay while he was doing it, who would deserve them more?

'Tell him it's no case for the pledge,' said Wrather. 'Tell him I'm past all that. And there's a certain amount of truth in that too. Say that I didn't drink fair. *He* didn't as a matter of fact: he wouldn't keep up. But say it was me. And say that I must be watched, and taught to drink at the same pace as other men, reasonable men like the Dean, I mean; or otherwise the black fellow will get me. And I shouldn't be surprised if he did in any case. But that's neither here nor there. You get him drinking level with me, and we'll soon bring out the dog in him, and we'll have a whale of an evening.'

It wasn't quite the way to talk; but I agreed. And I would have agreed to odder arrangements than that in the interests of science.

A few days later I had a talk with the Dean in the club, on the lines that Wrather and I had arranged.

'I am a good deal worried about that man Wrather,' I said.

'He is a bit crude, somewhat uncouth, somewhat perhaps . . .' said Dean Spanley.

And while he pondered some exacter word, I broke in with, 'It's worse than that. The man of course will never be a teetotaller, but he does not notice what other men drink, reasonable men I mean. His only chance would be to learn how much wine can be taken in safety.'

'That's not always so easy to teach, in a case like that,' said the Dean.

'No,' I said, 'and I have come to you for advice about it, for I shouldn't like to see Wrather, or any man, utterly ruined, as he soon must be if he goes on like that. What I thought was that if he could be guided by some sensible man, he might learn what was good for him and limit himself to that.'

'How do you mean?' said the Dean.

'Well, drinking glass for glass,' I said. 'I would see that the wine was passed round continually, and that each man had only his share.'

'H'm,' said the Dean.

'It's a rare wine, you see, and he's unfamiliar with it; and he'd learn, that way, how much he could take in safety. It might save him altogether.'

But still the Dean seemed suspicious, or at any rate not quite satisfied.

'I take it you can do that yourself,' he said.

It was then that I played, if I may say so, my master-stroke.

'I'm afraid not,' I said.

'Eh?' said the Dean.

'I am afraid,' I said, 'where so much is at stake for Wrather, I could not select myself as the perfect mentor.'

'I see,' said the Dean.

He remembered the occasion when I had given way to Tokay, a surrender by no means enforced on me, but still a surrender.

'Of course if you think he can be checked and brought round, in that way,' said the Dean; 'and I dare say it may not be impossible; then of course you should be very careful how it is done.'

'That is why I have come to you,' I said.

'To me, eh?'

'Yes.'

Things hung in the balance then, while the Dean pondered.

"I don't see how giving him more wine can teach him to take less,' he said; but there was doubt in his voice.

'If one tried to stop a case like that from taking any wine at all, one would lose the last vestige of influence over him, and he would be utterly lost. It's worth trying.'

'Oh, I suppose so,' said the Dean, and without enthusiasm, for Wrather had been distinctly rude to him.

And then I flashed out on him the ace of trumps. 'You suppose so! Can you doubt, Mr Dean, that any soul is worth saving?'

The ace of trumps at his own game, and it had to take the trick.

'I will certainly be glad to try,' he said.

So I arranged what at one time I had thought to have been impossible, another dinner at my house, at which Dean Spanley was to meet Wrather.

Then I went off to tell Wrather what I had done, and to book him for the date. And at the same time I tried, as tactfully as I could, to check in advance any levity in remarks he might make to the Dean.

'You've got to damned well save my soul,' said Wrather. 'Never mind about anything else.'

'You'll bring him right back with a jerk,' I said, 'if you talk like that when he's there. The split infinitive alone would be almost enough to do it.'

But all Wrather said was: 'We'll have him so far under, that nothing will bring him back.'

It is almost inconceivable to me, looking back on it, that such talk should have been the preliminary of a research of the first importance.

CHAPTER TEN

It was exactly as Wrather had said, when the dinner came off; he did lead the Dean to the point which we both of us, for very different reasons, desired: and to-day with all its trappings; sights, noises and points of view; fell away from him with the sudden completeness of snow on a southern slope, when the spring sun charms it thence and the sleeping grass is laid bare. At a certain stage of our dinner, and evidently just the right one, I had referred to his reminiscences. And at that moment I had addressed him not as Mr. Dean, but by his earlier name of Wag. Just plain Wag.

'As soon as they brought me round from my own house,' said the Dean, 'I used to have breakfast. And after that I used to run round to look for some food, in various places I knew of. There was the pig-sty for one. A very greedy devil, the pig, and a lot of good stuff was brought to him; and, if one knew just where to look, there was always a lot of it to be found that had slopped over into the mud; and even when one found nothing to get one's teeth into, there was always a very meaty taste in the water of all the puddles round there. And then there was a heap near the stables where a lot of good things were put. Various places, you know. On a lucky day I would sometimes eat till dinner-time; then have dinner, and go out to look for a bit more. That is one way of eating, and a very satisfying way. Another way is to hunt your own game and eat it nice and hot. They say it gives one an appetite; which of course it does; but there is no need for that; one always has an appetite. Still, life would not be complete without hunting. Hunting and dog-fighting should be one's main pursuits, as guarding is a duty, and eating a pastime.

'I shouldn't like you to go away with the idea, by the way, that I would eat anything. That was not so. One had a certain position to keep up, and a certain (shall I say?) dignity to preserve; and to preserve it I made a point of never eating bread. There were those that offered it to me, until they got to know me, but I always had to leave it on the carpet. There is no harm in bread, yet it has not only no flavour, but is one of those things that do not develop a flavour even when buried for a long time, so that it can never become interesting. To be a bread-eater is to my mind to be lacking in refinement or self-respect. I do not of course refer to soft toast, on which perhaps a snipe has been lying, all saturated with gravy: such things may be very precious.

'And cake of course is never to be confused with bread; it has a similar taste and the same disabilities, but is a far more important food, so that there can never be any loss of dignity in eating a piece of cake. The Wise Ones eat cake by itself, but to bread they always add something before eating it, which shows the unimportance of bread. And from this I come to table manners. One should catch one's food as neatly as possible. By fixing one's eyes on the Wise Ones before they throw, it is almost impossible to miss.'

Wrather moved slowly nearer to me, sideways. I knew what he was going to say.

'Do you think,' he whispered, 'that the old dog would catch anything now?'

I could not explain to Wrather at this time what in any case I had led him to believe was not the case, that this was research work on my part, not mere amusement. So all I said to him was, 'Don't whisper;' a rudeness that he forgave me at once with a twinkling eye.

'Eh? What?' said the Dean. 'I was saying that one should fix one's eyes on the Wise Ones. There are those that do not appreciate intense devotion at meal-times. But it is not for us to withhold our devotion on that account. It is born in all of us, and increased by beatings. A few sharp words should not diminish it. And sometimes it brings us abundant bones.'

'I say,' said Wrather, 'the old dog wants bucking up a bit.'

'Don't!' I said in an undertone. 'You'll bring him round.'

'No I shan't,' said Wrather. And to the Dean he said, 'Did you never have any more exciting experiences?'

'Exciting?' replied the Dean. 'Life is full of excitement, except while one is sleeping.'

'Anything specially thrilling, I mean,' said Wrather.

I couldn't stop him. But Dean Spanley, far from being brought back by him to our own time leaned forward and looked at Wrather, and said: 'I was out for a walk by myself, and I saw a nursery-maid and two children and a dog coming my way; and a strange new smell ran past me, and I glanced up and saw the look in the eyes of the dog. And I ran. I started just in time and he never came after me. It was rabies. And the nursery-maid and the children came quietly on, walking as they do on a Sunday.'

'Rabies!' said Wrather, all hushed. 'How did you know?'

'How did I know?' said the Dean. 'I saw his eyes. And the look was there.'

'And you couldn't have been mistaken?' I asked.

'It was glaring,' replied the Dean.

And that was one thing I learnt from him.

Wrather drank off a whole glass of Tokay, and said: 'Tell us something more cheerful.'

I was afraid every moment that Wrather would bring him back.

'Down,' I said to Wrather, who understood what I meant; and the sharp command helped, I think, to keep the Dean where he was among his old memories. Nevertheless he answered Wrather, and seemed to do what he asked.

'I remember the hounds coming once to our house; professional hunters, you know. I should have liked to have asked them whether they had been permitted to come there by the wise master, and whether their intentions were entirely correct, and indeed a great many other things; and, if their answers had been satisfactory, I should have liked to have told them all about our woods and all about who lived in them. I could have helped them in hundreds of ways. But unfortunately I was shut up. I shouted a good deal to them from my house; but I should have liked to have gone with them and showed them the way; I should have liked to have gone round and see that they were all quite well. And I should have liked to have chased the horses, so that they should not think, on account of their size, that they were more important than me. But there it was; I was shut up.

'I had an enormous amount to do when they left. I had to go and find out who they all were, and where they had come from, and if they were all quite well. Every tuft of grass had news of them. There were the scents of the hounds themselves, and scents from the roads they had come by, and tracks and scents of the horses: the field in front of our house was nothing less than a history; and it took me a long time to go through it. I was a bit behindhand owing to having been shut up, but scents that had gone from lawns and paths still hung in the taller grasses, and I was able to gather all the information that I required.'

'What for?' blurted out Wrather, before I could stop him.

'To guard the house,' said the Dean. 'It was my duty to guard it. And I had to know who had come near it, and what their business was. Our house was sacred, and we couldn't have people coming near it unless we knew what they had come for: there might have been an enemy among them. You will not suggest, I trust, that anybody and everybody should be allowed without enquiry, and without the most careful enquiry, near a sacred house.'

'Not at all,' said Wrather.

And I felt it necessary to add: 'Of course not.'

'Ours was a particularly sacred house,' said the Dean, still somewhat nettled. 'Even the butcher's cart had to be barked at, though at many houses such a cart as that would be allowed to drive up without question. I certainly could not have all those people coming without enquiring into their motives, and, as a matter of general interest, their state of health. So I naturally had a very busy morning. They went visiting in our wood while I was still shut up, and I heard them leave the wood hunting. They all shouted out that they were after a fox, and quite right too, but I could not allow them merely on that account to come near a house such as ours without proper investigations.

'And there were two or three light carriages that had come to our stables, and that were fortunately still there when I was let out. So I sniffed at the wheels to get news of what was going on in the world, and I left a message with all of them to say that I was quite well.'

CHAPTER ELEVEN

One more story we got from the Dean that night; he had met his friend again, the one that lived three overs away; he had come to the house we had heard of, running behind his cart. The Dean had gone up to him at once, or Wag, I should say, no doubt putting his nose right up to the other dog's, and flicking it away and trotting off, and the other dog had followed.

'I invited him to come hunting,' said the Dean, 'and he said he would like to, and we went off at once.'

'What was your friend's name?' put in Wrather.

'Lion-hunter,' replied the Dean.

'Did he hunt lions?' asked Wrather.

'No,' said the Dean, 'but he was always ready to, he was always expecting a lion in his garden, and he thought of himself as Lion-hunter, therefore it was his name.'

'Did you think of yourself as Wag?' asked Wrather, not in any way critically, but only, I think, to get the details right.

'No,' said the Dean, 'I answered to it. I came to them when the Great Ones called that name. I thought of myself as Moon-chaser. I had often hunted the moon.'

'I see,' said Wrather.

And he had spoken so suavely that he never brought the Dean round, as I feared a jarring note might have done.

'When we came to the wood,' continued the Dean, 'we examined several rabbit-holes; and when we came to a suitable one, a house with only two doors to it, and the rabbit at home, I set Lion-hunter to dig, and stood myself at the back-door. He did all the barking, while I waited for the rabbit to come out. Had the rabbit come out I should have leaped on him and torn him to pieces, and eaten up every bit, not allowing Lion-hunter or anyone in the world to have a taste of it. When my blood is up no one can take anything from me, or even touch it. I should have caught it with one leap, and killed it with one bite, and eaten even the fur. Unfortunately the rabbit lived deeper down than we thought.

'But it was not long before a very strange and beautiful scent blew through the wood, on a wind that happened to come that way from the downs outside. We both lifted our noses, and sure enough it was a hare. We ran out of the wood, and we very soon saw him; he was running over the downs on three legs, in that indolent affected manner that hares have. He stopped and sat up and looked at us, as though he hadn't expected to meet two great hunters. Then he went on again. We raced to a point ahead of him, so as to meet him when he got there, and we soon made him put down that other hind leg. Unfortunately before he got to the point that we aimed at, he turned. This happened to leave us straight behind him. We shouted out that we were hunting him, and that we were great hunters, Lion-hunter and I, and that nothing ever escaped from us, and that nothing ever would. This so alarmed him that he went faster. When he came to a ridge of the downs he slanted to his left, and we slanted more, so as to cut him off; but when we got over the ridge he had turned again. We shouted to him to stop, as it was useless to try to escape from us; but the tiresome animal was by now some way ahead. He had of course the white tail that is meant to guide us, the same as the rabbit has; and we kept him in sight for a long while. When he was no longer in sight we followed the scent, which Lion-hunter could do very well, though he was not as fast as I; and it led us to places to which I had never been before, over a great many valleys. We puzzled out the scent and followed on and on, and we did not give up the hunt until all the scent had gone, and nothing remained except the smell of the grass, and the air that blew from the sheep. Night came on rather sooner than usual, and we did not know where we were, so we turned for home.'

'How did you do that,' asked Wrather, 'if you did not know where you were?'

'By. turning towards it,' replied the Dean. 'I turned first, and then Lion-hunter turned the same way.'

'But. how did you know which way to turn?' persisted Wrather.

'I turned towards home,' said the Dean.

There was something here that neither Wrather nor I ever understood, though we talked it over afterwards, and I was never able to get it from the Dean. My own impression is that there was something concerned which we should not have understood in any case, however it had been explained. My only contribution to any investigation that there may be on these lines is merely that the queer thing is there: what it is I have failed to elucidate.

'We turned towards home,' the Dean went on, 'and that led us past a lot of places I never had seen before. We passed a farm where strange people barked at us; and we met a new animal, with a beard and a fine proud smell. The question arose as to whether we should hunt him, but he lowered his horns at us, and jumped round so quickly that the horns were always pointing the wrong way. So we decided we would not hunt him, and told him we would come and hunt him some other day, when it was not so late and we had more time; and we went on towards home. Presently we saw a window shining at us, and it did not look right. It was a small house and all shut up, and it looked as though bad people might be hiding in it. I asked Lion-hunter if we should go up to the house and bark at them; but he thought that they might be asleep, and that it was better to let bad people go on sleeping. So we went by the lighted window, but it looked very bad in the night. Then the moon came over the ridge of the downs, but not large enough to be barked at. And then we came to a wood, and it turned out to be our own wood. And we ran down the hill and came to my house and barked under the window. And Lion-hunter said that he thought he would go back to his own house now, in case our door should open and anyone come out of it angry. And I said that that might be best. And the door opened, and a Great One appeared. And I said that I had been hunting and that I never would hunt again, and that I had stayed out much much too late, and that the shame of my sin was so great that I could not enter the house, and would only just crawl into it. So I crawled in and had a beating, and shook myself, and it was a splendid evening. I laid down in front of the fire and enjoyed the warmth of it, and turned over the memory of our hunt slowly in my mind; and the fire and my memories and the whole of the night seemed brightened by my beating. How beautiful the fire was! Warmer than the sun, warmer than eating can make you, or running or good straw, or even beatings, it is the most mysterious and splendid of all the powers of Man. For Man makes fire with his own hand. There is no completer life than lying and watching the fire. Other occupations may be as complete, but with none of them do the glow, the warmth and the satisfaction that there are in a fire come to one without any effort of one's own. Before a fire these things come merely by gazing. They are placed in the fire by Man, in order to warm dogs, and to replenish his own magical powers. Wherever there is a fire there is Man, even out of doors. It is his greatest wonder. On the day that he gives to dogs that secret, as he one day will, dogs and men shall be equal. But that day is not yet. I stray a little, perhaps, from my reminiscences. These things are taught, and are known to be true, but they are not of course any part of my personal observations.'

'Who discovered that?' said Wrather before I could stop him.

'We do not know,' said the Dean.

'Then how do you know it's true?' asked Wrather.

'They shall be equal one day, and on that day,' said the Dean.

'What day?' asked Wrather.

'Why, the day on which Man tells dogs the secret of fire,' I said to end the discussion.

'Exactly,' said the Dean.

I frowned at Wrather, for we were getting near something very strange; and though Wrather's interruption did not bring the Dean back, as I feared every moment it might, we heard no more of that strange belief from him. He talked of common things, the ordinary experiences of a dog on a rug at the fireside; things that one might have guessed; nothing that it needed a spiritual traveller to come from a past age to tell us.

CHAPTER TWELVE

I pass over many weeks, weeks that brought no
success to my investigations. A feeling that I had
sometimes come very near to strange discoveries
only increased my disappointment. It seemed to
me that a dog had some such knowledge of the
whereabouts of his home as the mariner has of
the North Pole. The mariner knows by his com-
pass: how does the dog know? And then I had
gathered from the Dean that a dog can detect
rabies in another dog, before any signs of it
appear to the eyes of men. How was that done?
What a valuable discovery that might be, if only I
could follow it up. But I had no more than a hint
of it. And then the strange faith of which the
Dean had said only one or two sentences. All the
rest that I had got was no more than what an
observant man taking notes might have found

out or guessed about dogs; but these three things beckoned to me, promising something far more, like three patches of gold on far peaks in some El Dorado of knowledge. The lure of them never left me. I had long talks with Wrather. I let him see that it was more to me than a mere matter of amusement; and he stuck to me and promised to do what he could. He and the Dean and I dined together again, and Wrather and I did our utmost; but I began to see that, in spite of those lapses, induced partly by the rarity of the wine and mainly by the perseverance of deliberate efforts to lure him away from sobriety, the Dean was an abstemious man. Only at the end of our dinner for three or four minutes he stepped back into that mid-Victorian age, that he seemed able to enter in memory when the glare of to-day was dimmed for him; and the things that he said were trivial, and far from the secrets I sought. Nor were they the sort of things that one much cared to hear: there are many habits and tricks we forgive to dogs on account of their boundless affection, which somehow jar when heard from the lips of a dean. Once more we dined together, and at that dinner the Dean said nothing that would have surprised the timidest of any flock that he had ever tended. And next day Wrather told me definitely that he could do no more with the Dean.

'I won't say he's a teetotaller,' said Wrather, 'because I wouldn't say that lightly of any man, and I know he is not; but he has a damned strong tendency that way. We have got him over it once or twice, but he'll develop it yet. I can do no more with him.'

Not the way to talk; but never mind that: so much was at stake.

'What's to be done?' I said desperately.

'I'll help you all I can,' said Wrather, 'but it's only fair to tell you when I can do no more. He's not the right sort of fellow. He may have taken his whack once or twice like a sportsman, but it wasn't because he wanted to. It was just by accident, because he didn't know the strength of the booze. There are not many people that do. You want to be an emperor of Austria to gauge the strength of Tokay to a nicety.'

'Then I shall never find out what I'm after,' I said in despair.

'I wouldn't say that,' said Wrather. 'I'm not the only sportsman in the world. You want to find someone who takes a stiffer whack than I do, and takes it in a brighter way. There are men you can't help taking a glass with.'

For a moment I feared that such a quest was hopeless, till I suddenly thought of the Maharajah. It was said of him that champagne was to him what Vichy water is to some people; and, if a sportsman were needed, it was said too that even India had scarcely a score who might claim to be greater sportsmen. Moreover he knew so much of the situation already, that nothing would have to be explained to him. He was the very man.

'What about the Maharajah of Haikwar?' I said.

'He's a good sportsman,' said Wrather.

'You know him?' I asked.

'No,' said Wrather, 'but of course I've heard of him. And he might do.'

'I don't want stuff about lying in front of the fire,' I said. 'I want to find out how dogs can find their way home, by a new route and from a strange country. And I want to know how they can detect rabies long before we can; and one or two other things.'

'You'll have to get him deeper, for all that,' said Wrather; 'deeper than I've been able to get him. It's all very well for a dull old dog like the

Dean to lay down the exact number of glasses at which one ought to stop; and he's been doing a good deal of stopping just lately; but the fact remains that when you have a real bright sportsman like the Maharajah of Haikwar taking a glass or two of wine with a man, he does follow along a bit. He'll get him further than I ever got him.'

'Do you think so?' I said.

'I'm sure of it,' said Wrather. 'It's like horses out hunting. There's no horse living that would stand perfectly still and watch the field galloping away from him, however dull and slow he was. You'll see when the Maharajah comes. Ask me too and I'll do my bit, and we'll drag the Dean along yet.'

'Further than he's been hitherto?' I asked.

'The man's human after all,' said Wrather.

And somehow, from the way he spoke, I hoped again.

The next thing was to get the Maharajah. I called on his secretary, Captain Haram Bhaj, to ask if he and the Maharajah would come and dine with me. 'The fact is,' I said, 'that the proof of one of the principal tenets of his religion, and yours, is at stake. A friend of mine has a memory of a former incarnation. I will get him to come to the dinner. And if we can get him to speak, we may have inestimable revelations that may be of the utmost value to all of your faith.'

'Of course what His Highness is really interested in,' said Captain Haram Bhaj, 'is his handicap.'

'His handicap,' I lamely repeated.

'At polo,' said Haram Bhaj.

'But surely,' I said, 'his religion must mean something to him.'

'Oh yes,' said Haram Bhaj. 'Only, polo is His Highness's first interest.'

And then I thought of Wrather.

'I have a friend.' I said, 'who used to play a good deal of polo once. It would be a great pleasure to him to meet the Maharajah sahib, if His Highness will come and dine with me.'

Wrather had not actually spoken to me of polo, but I had a kind of feeling about him, which turned out to be right, that he had been a polo-player. When Captain Haram Bhaj saw that polo was likely to be the topic at dinner he said that he thought the Maharajah would come. And as it turned out he did. I warned Wrather about the polo, and a few nights later we were all gathered at my table, the Maharajah of Haikwar, Captain

Haram Bhaj, Wrather and I and the Dean; the first four of these resolved to rob the fifth of a secret that might justify the hope of the East and astound Europe.

CHAPTER THIRTEEN

Dean Spanley was asking the Maharajah of Haikwar about ancient customs in India; about Indian music, Indian dress and the tribes that live in the jungle. Wrather was talking to the Maharajah upon his other side, whenever he got an opportunity, about polo. And Haram Bhaj was watching.

Wrather had contributed to our efforts with one splendid remark that he had made to the Dean before the Indians arrived. 'In the East they think it a discourtesy if all the guests at a party do not drink glass for glass.'

The remark created the perfect atmosphere in which the Maharajah's efforts and mine would have the best chance of thriving, The Dean had drawn me aside and said: 'Is this good for Mr Wrather?' And I had said: 'Yes, it is ideal for him.

The Maharajah never goes one drop beyond what a man should.'

So now the plot was in progress with every chance of success. A base plot, some may say. Perhaps all plots are base. But look what there was at stake: a secret to which champagne and Tokay were the only keys. And what a secret! I felt that the world was waiting expectant outside the door.

We were all drinking champagne. Tokay was to come at the end as a *coup de grâce*. I flatter myself that the champagne was of a good vintage; and the evening progressed to a point at which the Maharajah laid bare his heart and told Wrather the ambition of his life. I do not think that with an oriental you always get a clear sight of his innermost feelings, but I think that it was so with the Maharajah of Haikwar. His ambition was to have a handicap of nine at polo. At present he was only eight. And as yet the Dean had not spoken at all of anything nearer himself than the customs of Indian villages.

There was no servant in the room; my butler had gone to bed; and we passed round the champagne among ourselves. Haram Bhaj was particularly helpful. And the Dean was holding back all

the time. Yet that force was present that is sometimes found at the pastime of table turning, when
everybody combines to pull the same way; and
though Dean Spanley set himself against this
force, he gradually went with it. More and more I
felt that the world was hushed and waiting. And
then with the first glass of the Tokay he spoke,
spoke from that other century and sojourn. The
Maharajah looked interested. But as yet nothing
came that was stranger than what we had already
heard, nothing that is not known or could not be
guessed among those that have carefully studied
the ways of dogs. I passed round more Tokay, and
the Maharajah and Haram Bhaj and Wrather
helped me. The Dean was telling a story about a
dog-fight, not greatly different from the one that I
have already given my reader. As in the former
one he had gone for the ear, and had succeeded
in getting the grip, and brought that tale to a close
with a good deal of boasting. It was without doubt
a dog that was speaking to us, but a dog with nothing to tell us we did not know. I tried yet more
Tokay, and everyone helped me. We got a little
idyll then of a spring morning some decades back
into the century that is gone; not very interesting,
except for the shining eyes of the Dean as he told

it, and not very seemly. The stock of Tokay was running low, but was equal to one grand effort: we were all drinking it now in claret glasses. And suddenly I felt that the moment was hovering when what I waited for would be revealed, something that Man could not know unless told like this; and I knew that Dean Spanley's secrets were about to be laid bare.

I knew that the Maharajah cared more for his handicap than for those religious tenets that he mainly left to the Brahmins, and that the interest he had shown already was little more than the interest that he took as a sportsman in dog-fights; but now that the moment was coming for which I had waited so long I held up my hand to hush them, and as a sign that the mystery of which I had spoken was going to be shown to us now. And so it was. And so it was.

Everything I had sought was laid bare with open hands. I learned the faith of the dog; I knew how they see rabies in the eyes of another long before men guess it; I knew how dogs go home. I knew more about scent than all the Masters of Hounds in England have ever guessed, with all their speculations added together. I knew the wonderful secrets of transmigration. For half an hour that evening I might have spoken with Brahmins, and they would at least have listened to what I had to say, without that quiet scorn lying under a faint smile, with which they listen to all else that we may say to them. For half an hour I knew things that they know. Of this I am sure.

And now my readers will wish to hear them too. Be not too hard on me, reader. It is no easy thing to make a dean drunk. For a cause less stupendous I should not have attempted it. I attempted it for a secret unknown to Europe; and with the help of the Maharajah and the two others, drinking glass for glass, I accomplished it. All that I remember. What Dean Spanley said after his tale of the dog-fight and his little love-affair, I do not remember. I know that he held the key to some strange mysteries, and that he told us all. I remember the warm room and the lighted candles, and light shining in the champagne and in the Tokay, and people talking, and the words 'Never trust a teetotaller or a man who wears elastic-sided boots.' Then I noticed that a window was open, and some of the candles were out and all the rest were low, and everybody seemed to have gone. I went to the window then and leaned out to refresh myself, and when I came back to my chair,

I kicked against a body on the floor and found that Wrather was still there, partly under the table. The Maharajah and Haram Bhaj and the Dean were gone. And I propped up Wrather against the legs of a chair, and after a while he spoke. And he said: 'For God's sake give me a whisky and soda. No more Tokay. For God's sake a whisky and soda.'

And I gave him a whisky and soda, and that brought him round, and I took a little myself. And his first words after that were: 'Well, we got the old dog to talk.'

'Yes,' I said. 'What did he say?'

'That's what I can't remember,' he said.

And that was my trouble too.

I gave Wrather a bed, and I went to bed myself, and in the morning our memories were no clearer.

Knowing the enormous importance of what was said, I went round after a light breakfast to see Haram Bhaj. He had been to Vine Street and stayed there the night, and they had let him go in the morning; and the only clue he had to what he had heard overnight was that he had told the inspector at Vine Street that he, Haram Bhaj, was a black-and-grey spaniel and could get home by himself.

'Now why did I say that?' he said.

But there was not enough in that to be of any use whatever; and later in the day I called on the Maharajah.

'It was a very jolly evening,' he said; and he was evidently grateful to me. But after a while I saw that I should lose his attention unless I talked of polo. Either he remembered nothing, or the secrets of transmigration, if they were secrets from him, scarcely attracted his interest, and he left all such things to the Brahmins.

It only remained to try Dean Spanley again, and this I shall never do now. For very soon after that dinner the Dean was promoted to bishop. He still knows me, still greets me, whenever we meet at the club. But I shall never get his secret. One of the shrewdest observers of the last century, the lady after whom the greater part of that hundred years was named, stated in one of her letters that she had never known a man who became a bishop to be quite the same as he was before. It was so with Dean Spanley. I can remember no act or word of his that ever showed it, and yet I have sufficiently felt the change never to trouble him with invitations to dine with me any more.

Wrather and I often dined together and, I trust, will often again. We feel like travellers who once, for a short while, have seen something very strange; and neither of us can remember what it was.

Left Horatio Fisk finds his interest waning, as his son Henslowe reads to him in his study.

Below Henslowe steels himself for his weekly audience with his father.

Right Henslowe discusses his difficult father with Mrs Brimley, Fisk Snr's housekeeper.

Above The Nawab's mansion, at which is to be held a lecture on The Transmigration of Souls(*left*).

Below The Nawab spends his days playing cricket.

Above The Swami begins his lecture.

Above The Fisks and their new acquaintance, Mr Wrather, are not a captive audience. . .

Right . . .whereas Dean Spanley has a particular interest in the subject.

Above Cat? What cat?

Above The Dean is not very enthusiastic about Fisk Jnr's invitation to dinner.

Right Henslowe begins his search for a bottle of the Dean's favourite tipple, Imperial Tokay.

Above Wrather locates a bottle of the precious drink in the cellar vaults.

Above The Dean is most impressed with the vintage, and the aroma.

Whilst walking around the
cathedral, tension between
father and son grows.

Right Dean Spanley
is uncomfortable with
Wrather joining them
for dinner.

Below The price of Wrather's
help is an invitation to meet
Dean Spanley. But he is
unconvinced by the Dean's
recollections – at first. . .

Below Wrather drives
Fisk Jnr back with a case
of the Nawab's Tokay, in
preparation for a dinner
party at Fisk Snr's house.

Left Wag greets a visitor (*far left*), who promises excitement and adventure beyond the gates of his master's house.

Below The adventure begins!

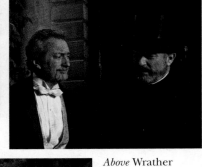

Above Fisk Snr and Mrs Brimley remember his fallen son, Harrington.

Above Wrather offers to walk with the Dean, to see that he gets home safely.

Left Fisk Snr makes the acquaintance of a new friend.

The Film

INTRODUCTION

Appropriately enough, *My Talks With Dean Spanley* began life at a dinner party, almost eight years ago. New Zealand-born producer Matthew Metcalfe was visiting a friend, when he slapped a short script on the table, penned by Scottish screenwriter Alan Sharp (best known for *Rob Roy*), and asked Metcalfe to take a look. It was an adaptation of *My Talks With Dean Spanley*, a novella by Anglo-Irish writer Lord Dunsany, published back in 1936. Metcalfe read the script, and thought it was amazing, but it was fifty pages long and there wasn't really anything that could be done with it from a commercial point of view.

While many novellas lend themselves automatically to feature film adaptation, *My Talks With Dean Spanley* was structured around a series of dinners between the titular Dean and the story's narrator,

Henslowe Fisk, during which the former recounts his life as a dog in a previous existence. That is where the book begins and ends, but to expand the story Metcalfe and Sharp decided there had to be a reason why Fisk was continuing with his dinners with the Dean. Finally they concluded that maybe he was doing it because he wants to understand something important to him – that he was reaching out. That's when the idea of the father came up.

Enter the character of Horatio Fisk, who had not featured in Lord Dunsany's original. As Sharp's script reflects, it's his strained relationship with his son, the narrator, which helps form the emotional arc of the film. Thus reincarnation is swapped for reconciliation. It now reflected the situation where every father has, at some point, struggled to understand his son, while every son has struggled to understand his father. It was about how sons feel when their fathers don't say they approve of them, or they appreciate them, or that they love them, or that they think they're worthy. It's about how fathers seem to struggle to communicate this to their sons, and how sons don't feel they can pull their fathers up on this.

In November 2006 Metcalfe received a copy of Sharp's script – still missing the final thirty or so pages but now definitely shaped like a feature – and decided to proceed. With the title now shortened to *Dean Spanley*, Metcalfe teamed up with UK producer Alan Harris and decided to set up an Anglo-New Zealand co-production to fund the film. The next few months were spent finding the finances, while Harris and Metcalfe decided on who should direct *Dean Spanley*.

Metcalfe felt very strongly that *Dean Spanley* should be told by someone who understood families. As much as it is a comedy, and it is wry, dry and acerbic, and eccentric, it is also possessed of a lot of heart. It was decided to go with the New Zealand-raised director Toa Fraser, an emerging talent whose 2006 debut, *No.2*, won the prestigious Audience Award at the Sundance Film Festival, and which revealed someone who really understood human beings and the way they communicate.

Sent the script, Fraser read it and responded immediately. But for a script so dialogue-driven, he knew the casting process would be critical. From the outset he stated that he didn't want to make it without a very good cast, and he got his wish, drawing on the crème-de-la-crème of talent from New Zealand, Australia and Britain. The first on board was Bryan Brown, the veteran Australian-born star of such films as *Cocktail* and *Gorillas in the Mist*. He was cast as the Australian entrepreneur Wrather, who befriends Henslowe Fisk and helps him lure the Dean into further revelatory dinners. In Brown's words: 'He can hustle up things. He calls himself a middle man or a facilitator. In other words, he intends to do well and he's happy to get in and graft.'

At this point, the attention turned to the casting of Horatio Fisk. Metcalfe, along with Harris and Fraser, decided to 'dare to dream' and send it to eight-time Oscar nominee Peter O'Toole, who had also worked with Bryan Brown twenty-five years previously. Months went by, and Metcalfe was actually filming a documentary in Northern Iraq when he managed to listen to his voicemails through a satellite phone; there was the hoped-for message: 'Peter is interested. He really likes the script. Is it still on offer...?'

As for O'Toole, reading *Dean Spanley*, and being reminded of its source writer, Lord Dunsany, was a blast from the past: 'I'd not heard of him for fifty years. I looked through his credits, and I remembered him for three works. I knew him as a short story writer and I knew him as a playwright, but not for fifty years had I even heard his name. An amazing man, as we now know – and a great chess champion!' He was also impressed with Alan Sharp's adaptation, calling it 'a most unusual script. It's different. I can't compare it with anything – except it's a sophisticated comedy of a high level.' O'Toole loved his time on the set, and summed up the story thus: 'Take away all the occult, all the transmigration, and what it is, is a father and a son who are estranged by events. It is truly just a reconciliation – and very beautiful and on a simple human level.'

For Fraser the chance to work with O'Toole, who was Oscar-nominated for his lead role in Roger Michell's *Venus*, was an intimidating task he took to with relish. Fraser described him as 'a man who is at the very peak of his capabilities. He knows completely what he can do with his face, with his voice, with his body, with his heart. You can whisper one word in his ear and it changes his performance completely. He can just do that. It gives him an idea and sends him spinning to a different nuanced performance that's really exciting, but at the same time keeps very faithful to making sure the scene and story works.'

For Jeremy Northam, he saw his character's journey in slightly different terms. 'I suppose he thinks he's doing something in order to lift his father out of his gloom, the stasis that he's in. But actually, the son is in his own gloom. He's in his own situation that he's trying to resolve. A lot of people, certainly by the time they reach a certain stage in life, have fairly complex relationships with their parents, if they're still around. But it seems that parents generally of a certain age don't say to their kids what they think of them. It's very easy for people to get crossed wires and the offspring to think that they're not cared for perhaps. And it's very easy for the parents to think that they're detested by the children. I think that's at the nub of their relationship.'

As the narrator of the piece, it meant that Northam was in virtually every scene – and was required to be on set for every moment of the 36-day shoot. With most of his lines spoken as voiceover, it meant Northam had less dialogue to learn than some of his peers, so he found his role a very reactive part.

Concurrent to the casting of Northam was the crucial selection of who to play Dean Spanley. Metcalfe says that there was only one name they ever talked about: Sam Neill. They never actually discussed another name and were unsure what they would have done if they didn't have him. Yet according to Harris, the New Zealand-raised star of such prestige projects as *Jurassic Park* and *The Piano* was not easy to get on board. He turned them down a couple of times, but they just kept going back at him.

In the end, Neill decided to take on the role, presumably – as an owner of three working vineyards himself – taken by the idea that Dean Spanley always begins his canine recollections after two glasses of the Hungarian sweet wine, imperial Tokay. It also undoubtedly helped that, not unlike his character, Neill is also a dog lover, owning a Staffordshire bull terrier of whom he is inordinately fond. It certainly helped with his preparation: 'What I've drawn on is embedded in myself: a familiarity with odd people and dogs!'

The biggest challenge for Neill was learning the lines. There was as much dialogue in this one film as he'd done in all the last five years. He recalls: 'It was very unusual in that respect, in that it's very dialogue heavy. It's all about ideas and stories.' In the final scene, for example, in which Dean Spanley recounts a crucial day in the life of his previous incarnation, he had to learn lines spanning some nineteen pages.

With the cast in place, Fraser and Metcalfe set about gathering the key heads-of-department. Not unsurprisingly, Fraser favoured a series of vastly experienced men and women, led by cinematographer Leon Narbey (*Whale Rider*), with whom he had worked on *No.2*. Also recruited was costume designer Odile Dicks-Mireaux, a three-time BAFTA TV nominee who had just come off Roland Emmerich's *10,000 BC*. For production design, he chose the Auckland-born Andrew McAlpine, who has worked with numerous top directors including Danny Boyle (*The Beach*), Spike Lee (*Clockers*) and Jane Campion (*The Piano*).

Filming began in November 2007, in several locations around Cambridgeshire and East Anglia, including Elm Hill in Norwich as well as the city's Cathedral's cloisters. By late January 2008, the production moved to New Zealand where the second unit material (scenes where Dean Spanley recalls his past life) was shot.

Unsurprisingly, numerous stately homes in England were taken full advantage of. With scenes also shot at Holkham Hall and Peckover House, one of the key locations was Elveden Hall, near Thetford, which has featured in numerous films, including Stanley Kubrick's *Eyes Wide Shut*. The setting for the lecture where all the characters first meet – a mansion house belonging to the cricket-mad Nawab of Ranjiput – it required a bowling strip to be built in the great hall. Fraser says that the hard thing was keeping Peter away from the cricket ball. He actually recommended the guys who play the extras in the scene and put the director in touch with the MCC.

It wasn't just Fraser's ability to work with crews from the other side of the world that was called upon. One of the principal reasons he was brought in is because his background in theatre. He is a playwright by profession so very good with actors. Utilising those skills, in regard to working with the cast, was very important, yet it was crucial – and the ambition of the team – to make such a dialogue-driven piece as cinematic as possible.

Getting the tone right was the biggest challenge. Bringing what Harris calls 'an adult fairy tale' to the screen meant striking a delicate balance between the serious and the comic. It is a surreal story, but they played it very, very straight. The characters are talking about reincarnation, something that is very bizarre, and they're believing it. What the film-makers tried to do, in regard to the way they shot it, was to lure the audience into a heightened sense of reality, so that they're more ready to accept this surreal idea that there is a Dean who is actually talking about his previous life as a dog.

As to the question of who the audience is for Dean Spanley, when they first started putting the project together it was aimed at the older generation. But as the film progressed it became clear that this is the kind of story that younger viewers could actually find very interesting. They could be quite enthralled by the subject matter, a man talking about his life as a dog. Yet if it's anything, Metcalfe believes it's the central relationship between the Fisks that will grab viewers. 'Film and literature is filled with father-son stories,' he concludes. '*Star Wars* is a father-son story, as crazy as it sounds. And that's what *Dean Spanley* is ultimately about – a father and a son bridging the gulf.'

DEAN SPANLEY

Screenplay by
ALAN SHARP

BASED ON THE NOVEL,
MY TALKS WITH DEAN SPANLEY
by Lord Dunsany

1 EXT. LANDSCAPE - EVENING

*A large honey-hued moon hoists itself above a wooded skyline.
We HEAR, running over the IMAGES, whose SEPIA TONES
suggest the early days of photographic discovery:*

NARRATOR (V.O.): This story began far ago and
long away, although I can only vouch for the part
I personally experienced, and even that part I
cannot claim to entirely understand, such is its
strange and improbable nature... I relate it now

in the hope that, whatever its other failings, it will convince even the most sceptical amongst you that it is never too late to meet one's father for the first time...

CUT TO:

2 EXT. GATE - EVENING

At the gate of what is evidently a substantial estate, a large country house set in extensive grounds, a BOY of 9 or 10 years, stands staring, watching, waiting, his whole manner that of anxious hope. A CALL reaches him from the house. He turns, looks back, then summoned again, reluctantly walks away from the gate, goes into the house.

CUT TO:

3 INT. BEDROOM - NIGHT

A SEQUENCE in which we see the Boy at the window of a child's bedroom, face close to the pane, and then when removed by some partially seen ADULT, seen kneeling at the foot of his bed in prayer; then in bed trying to sleep; then asleep, but waking up with a start and a cry; then back at the window, watching, and finally asleep, face pressed to the glass. All the while the MOON rises, its colour now a pitiless bone white.

The CAMERA LEAVES the Boy's face, DESCENDING FROM the window down the facade of the building, to find, in a TIME DISSOLVE:

4 EXT. HOUSE - MORNING

The Boy, dressed now is being seen off by SEVERAL ADULTS and a small GIRL, of 3 or 4 years. We should identify parents, a nanny and the domestics, all of whom display varying levels of concern for the obviously unhappy lad as he boards a pony and trap and is driven off, trying as best he can not to let his distress overflow into tears.

Only the little Girl is unaffected by the general melancholy as she waves, uncomprehendingly, as the pony and trap goes down the drive and runs after it, calling 'bye' until the Boy looks round, an expression of uncoverable loss on his face. It is enough to stop the little Girl, taking all the excitement out of her. She stands as the trap and its tragic passenger go on down the drive.

FADE TO BLACK:

RUN LEGEND: 65 YEARS LATER

DISSOLVE TO:

5 EXT. STREET - DAY - CREDITS

A terraced row of imposing townhouses, along which various FIGURES move: a NANNY with her charges; a delivery van, horse-drawn, sundry PEDESTRIANS, and, coming towards the CAMERA, our NARRATOR, a tall man in his somewhere forties. All of the above, by their garb, indicate the era to be the early years of the 20th century. Of the Narrator's clothes we should note he wears high collars, fashionable, but restrictive. We HEAR:

> **NARRATOR (V.O.):** It is a commonplace observation that remarkable events often have ordinary beginnings. Never was this more true than of my talks with Dean Spanley, which form the spine of our narrative. Properly speaking, they began on a Thursday, the day on which I visit my father, Mr Horatio Fisk. This habit, one might even say, ritual, commenced after the death of my younger brother, Harrington, in the Boer War, and the subsequent demise of my dear mama, occasioned by her grief at this unsupportable loss...

And he has come by now to a door where he rings the bell, waits, turns to survey the street. We sense someone, if not exactly steeling himself, certainly preparing for what lies

*ahead. After a moment, he rings the bell again, and we HEAR
a WOMAN'S VOICE from the interior calling, irritably,*

VOICE: I'm coming...I'm coming!

*And the door opens to reveal a WOMAN of the serving class,
animated and exasperated, staring out.*

NARRATOR (V.O.): How are you, Mrs Brimley...?

MRS BRIMLEY: As you see me. Could complain,
but what'd be the use of that...

The Narrator steps past her, and she closes the door.

6 INT. FISK'S HOUSE - DAY - CONTINUOUS

NARRATOR: Yes indeed...

Handing her his hat.

NARRATOR: ...and himself...?

Mrs Brimley sniffs the nasal equivalent of a shrug.

MRS BRIMLEY: Oh, he's working up a head of
steam...you know how he gets. Sent back the
Times, he did, to have it properly ironed...

She takes the hat to a closet, puts it away. Goes to the kitchen door, saying,

MRS BRIMLEY: ...I'm just finishing the obituaries. Give me a minute and you can take it in to him...

And the Narrator follows her into her spacious domain, where, saying,

NARRATOR: I thought he didn't read the obituaries..

7 INT. KITCHEN - DAY

The London Times *is spread, page by page on the table where Mrs Brimley has been ironing it. She returns to this task as the Narrator begins carefully to reassemble the sheets, glancing at them as he does.*

MRS BRIMLEY: No more he does, but he wants them ironed just the same...says he doesn't read them because he's afraid he'll come across his own name one day. I ask you...

Mrs Brimley wielding the smoothing iron, goes on, the Narrator smiling his smile, studies the page containing the adverts, noting among them one telling of a lecture by Swami Nala Prash on 'The Transmigration of Souls'.

MRS BRIMLEY: ...Used to be the first thing he turned to up until you-know-what...

And the Narrator clearly does know what, but seizes on the advert as a change of subject.

NARRATOR: Tell me, Mrs Brimley, do you believe in transmigration of souls?

MRS BRIMLEY: I'm not for letting foreigners come in, if that's what you mean...

NARRATOR: No, no, not immigration... re-incarnation. The belief that the immortal soul has many earthly homes...

MRS BRIMLEY: Never gave it much thought, I haven't...

She pauses and the Narrator picks up the re-assembled pristine paper. Then,

MRS BRIMLEY: ...After Albert died, I went to one of them mediums, but she couldn't get a hold of him... I wasn't surprised, mind you. He never said much when he were alive, Albert didn't. Couldn't imagine him piping up once he was dead. No, I think when the light goes out, that's more or less it. Mind you don't crease that now..

And the Narrator, minding the crease, turns to leave, as she goes on,

MRS BRIMLEY: ...He won't know what day it is, not having read the paper. You'll be a reminder, I daresay...

7A INT. HOUSE - DAY

The Narrator goes down the corridor to a door. Stops as if to compose himself and he runs a finger around his collar in a reflexive, involuntary easing motion. Then he knocks and goes in.

7B INT. STUDY - DAY

The room is a splendid one, running long and high to a set of windows that give on to a large, somewhat overgrown garden, but one that obviously has the potential for splendour.

A MAN sitting a winged-back chair looks up as the Narrator enters, a sharp, peevish expression surmounted by a halo of silver hair.

FISK: Ah, Young Fisk, must be Thursday...

As the Narrator walks towards him.

NARRATOR: It is indeed...

FISK: Very handy a Thursday, keeps Wednesday and Friday from colliding... that my *Times*?

The Narrator hands it over, looks out of the window as Fisk opens the pristine pages.

NARRATOR: You really should have the garden seen to, Father...

FISK: That was your mother's job...

The Narrator gives a little grimace, looks to the wall where an oil painting of a petite, once-pretty woman hangs, says,

NARRATOR: Nevertheless...

His father looks up at him, sharp, angered.

FISK: 'Nevertheless' what does that expression mean, I ask you. 'Never the less,' be as well clearing your throat for all the sense it makes..

And the Narrator turns, fingering his collar, changing the subject.

NARRATOR: It's a fine day, Father. Have you anything particular in mind?

FISK: I can see how fine the day is. As for 'particular in mind', everything is particular when you get down to it...

The Narrator has been down these byways before, says with patience,

NARRATOR: I mean, have you any plans, are there any concerts, exhibitions, parades, other diversions you'd like to attend...?

Tailing off. His father, looking through the paper, frowns, says,

FISK: There's nothing about the war...

NARRATOR: We are not presently at war, so far as I know...

FISK: That would explain it...

He finds the place he wants.

FISK: ...Diversions, you say. That's all that's left you know, before stepping out of the anteroom of eternity...

Said with no trace of self pity, frowning down at the page. Then,

FISK: There is a display of aboriginal weapons from our wars of imperial conquest...assegais, knob-kerries, boomerangs, blowpipes. Pitiful implements, one would imagine. Give the beggars Mausers, I say, let them play the White Man's game properly... And a showing of the water colours of one Euphemia Gallogolly entitled 'Nuances of Light,' and a sorry collection of spinsterly vapourings it will be, I have no doubt...

He shakes his head at the prospect, then, going on,

FISK: And an exhibition of Georgian shoe buckles. Over two thousand items. Now that was an era, when a gentleman could spend a fortune ornamenting his feet...

He looks up, suddenly.

FISK: Did we win the Boer War...?

NARRATOR: I believe we lost more slowly than the other side...

Fisk nods, stares out of the window a moment, frowning, then,

FISK: Garden never recovered from it...

Looking over his father's shoulder at the newspaper, the Narrator reads, pointing,

NARRATOR: How about the lecture by one Swami Nala Prash on the transmigration of souls...

FISK: Nonsense, if you ask me. No indication there's any such thing as a soul.

NARRATOR: Perhaps not, but it is a widely held belief of all the major religions.

FISK: Poppycock. You think if we had souls they wouldn't get in touch? 'Course they would. Think your mother wouldn't be on to me about that garden...

NARRATOR: Still, it sounds the most likely of the lot, don't you think?...

Fisk doesn't look too sure. He looks at the article, reading, then sees something that perks up his interest considerably.

FISK: Well, what do you know... It's being given at the home of the Nawab of Ranjiput... Isn't that the cricketing Indian chappie...?

NARRATOR: I believe so.

FISK: Heard tell he turned the ballroom into a cricket pitch...mad as badgers, most of those Nawabs... Get out the wheelchair, Young Fisk, we'll get some exercise...

CUT TO:

7C EXT. ROAD - DAY

A road leading into rural surroundings and the Narrator is pushing Fisk Sr along in the wheelchair, which is an impressive basketwork model and not light with it. They are figures in the landscape, and we HEAR:

FISK (V.O.): So how is it going...?

NARRATOR (V.O.): Very smoothly so far...

FISK (V.O.): As it should. Latest model guaranteed to outlast its user. Not that that's saying much...

NARRATOR (V.O.): Nonsense, Father, you have many miles left in you yet...

His voice just beginning to convey signs of effort.

CUT TO:

7D EXT. MANSION - DAY

The Narrator, now labouring, wheels his charge up a long drive towards a large, grandiose house. As they approach, an automobile of some sporting variety comes roaring up from BEHIND them, blows its horn, goes past, giving a glimpse of the DRIVER, be-goggled and helmeted.

The Narrator stops, glad of the rest while Fisk shakes a fist after the vehicle.

FISK: Damned machines, be the death of all, they will...

NARRATOR: Progress, Father, occasions certain inconveniences...

FISK: Push on, push on...

And they come in time up to the steps of the entrance. There is a CUSTODIAN at the door, ostentatious in turban and brocade jacket.

The car that went past is parked out front and the Driver is standing by it, taking off his helmet and goggles. The Narrator pushes Fisk up to the steps, looks down at him.

NARRATOR: We're here, Father...

FISK: Well, get me inside. Can't sit out here...

At that moment, the Driver leaves his car and is making up the steps. He stops, looks at them, and in a distinctly colonial accent, asks,

WRATHER: Want a hand with the buggy...?

Drawing a glare from Fisk.

NARRATOR: I'm sure the doorman will assist...

WRATHER: Catch a hold, we'll have it up in a jiff...

Seizing one wheel, causing the Narrator to take the other, and they lift the wheelchair and carry it up the steps. Then the man releases his hold, nods appreciatively.

WRATHER: Clyde built by the feel of it...

And goes off into the house, Fisk glaring after him.

FISK: Buggy indeed, damn cheek...

And the Narrator pushes him in, past the Doorman and a sign on an easel which says, 'The Transmigration of Souls. A modern assessment by Swami Nala Prash.'

10 INT. MANSION - DAY

Almost immediately inside the door, they are confronted by a cornucopia of exotic furnishings and mounted sporting trophies. Not content with the usual truncated triumphs of the hunt, heads, horns and antlers, the Nawab has the whole beast on display; lions, tigers, water buffaloes and even a crocodile, deport themselves in a large area inside the door.

A sign points them towards the back of the house and they follow it, passing as they do, the entrance into what evidently has been

*in another incarnation, a ballroom. It has now been made over
into a cricket strip on which a batsman, wicket keeper, bowler
and umpire are presently engaged in play. The batsman is the
NAWAB, a plump, moustached figure, padded up and wearing
a cap. The walls of the room display a diorama of the archetypical
village cricket scene complete with elms, rooks, a pavilion with a
clock showing the time at 2:50 pm, and a scattering of spectators.
Fisk stops to look in at this extravagant whimsy and the
Narrator joins him in time to see the Nawab comprehensively
bowled by a yorker.*

    FISK: Damn foolish game, cricket, if you ask me.
Too many rules...

And he gets out of the chair, and walks on. The Narrator lingers a moment, watches the Nawab walk away to scattered applause from the other participants. He goes into the 'Pavilion,' a door in the wall complete with three steps and a verandah. Then, a moment later he appears and comes jauntily back to the restored wicket and proceeds to take guard. The Narrator moves on after his father, pushing the wheelchair.

11 INT. LECTURE ROOM - DAY

He finds him surveying a space set with a dozen or so folding chairs of which only a few are in use. There are two LADIES sitting together, and at the back, near the door, a MAN with a clerical collar.

Fisk looks over the assembly and as the Narrator comes up to him, says,

FISK: Not exactly a full house, is it?

The Narrator is about to sit down near the back, but Fisk marches down to the front, sits immediately before the low dais which contains a large, throne-like wicker chair. Somewhat reluctantly, the Narrator follows him. The Driver who helped with the wheelchair is sitting a few seats over.

FISK: Want to be where we can see the yellow of his eyes...

And as the Narrator settles beside him, Fisk stares at the Driver, then looks around, barely glancing at the ladies who sit, heads together, talking in whispers. Then, noticing the CLERICAL FIGURE at the back who seems to be studying the ceiling moulding,

FISK: I declare, that's Spanley, the new Dean of St. Justus...

NARRATOR: Keep your voice down, Father.

The Driver leans across and says,

WRATHER: Dean Spanley, you say...?

FISK: Not me, the chap with the dog collar...

The Driver moves down to join them, conspiratorially,

WRATHER: What's a Dean doing at a sermon on reincarnation, is what I'd like to know...

FISK: Exactly my thought.

NARRATOR: I think it shows commendable open-mindedness...

FISK: Impending apostasy, more like. Seen the error of his Christian ways...

WRATHER: The name's Wrather, with a W...

FISK: Fisk.

WRATHER: And what brings you here, Mr Fisk?

FISK: Ask young Fisk. His idea...

Indicating the Narrator, who says,

NARRATOR: The lesser of several evils...

WRATHER: I know the Nawab. He asked me to come along to make up the numbers.

FISK: He should have asked more than you by the look of things.

At that moment a loud appeal is heard, followed by the same desultory clapping.

WRATHER: He's prone to leg before. Takes the wrong guard every time.

FISK: Damn foolish game. Too many rules.

WRATHER: It's what the English have instead of ethics...

The Narrator shoots him a glance and looks as if he might challenge the speaker, only to desist as the Nawab himself

COMES INTO the room, still in his cricket kit, bat under his arm, peeling off his gloves. He comes to the front, surveys the sparse audience without obvious signs of disappointment.

NAWAB: Well, there you are. I thought I got a thin edge onto my pad, but when the umpire raises his finger, you have to walk... that's life and cricket...

He whacks his bat on his pad for emphasis.

NAWAB: ...Well, then, time to bring on Swami Prash. Of what he will tell you today, I have no particular opinion, but I've always held him in high regard as a cricketer. Bowled decent left arm leg breaks before he went holy. Haven't seen him play since, but I've no doubt he's still the sportsman he was...

He repeats the leg whacking routine as a kind of punctuation.

NAWAB: ...Right, I'll let him wheel away. You should ignore any noises you hear during his discourse. Leather on willow, sweetest of all the man-made sounds, in my opinion. If you exclude the cork coming out of a magnum of Petrus...

And with another whack on his leg, he moves off, the two ladies venturing a discreet clapping that the Nawab raises his bat to before he exits.

Then the SWAMI comes in and down to the dais. He turns, faces them, makes the palms-pressed-together-little-bow greeting, peculiar to his profession, and takes his seat on the wicker throne. As he begins to speak in a mellifluous sing-song Indian English, we observe in necessary detail that his attire consists of a conservative business suit and elastic-sided boots.

SWAMI PRASH: The question of the transmigration of souls, perhaps more familiarly known to you as reincarnation, has been a structural underpinning of Indian philosophical and religious thought for

millennia. Only recently, through the work of certain European pioneers has this esoteric wisdom come to the attention of the Western mind...

At a certain point the Swami's VOICE FADES OUT and we HEAR:

NARRATOR (V.O.): I confess the appearance of Swami Prash came as something of a surprise, even a disappointment, for although I had no clear expectation of what a holy man would look like, I had imagined one with such a title and discussing such a subject, would be dressed more traditionally...

At the end of this speech, the Swami's VOICE FADES UP again:

SWAMI PRASH: ...It is my hope today, in the time allotted me, to bring these two mind sets a little, if only a little, closer...

And we HEAR, as the Swami's VOICE AGAIN FADES OUT:

NARRATOR (V.O.): He proved prophetic in this last modest assessment, for what ensued proved to be as un-illuminating a fifty minutes as I can remember spending outside the confines of Parliamentary debate...

We see, in a SERIES OF DISSOLVES, his father begin to nod off and fall to a gentle snoring; Wrather begin to fidget and roll his eyes; and the two ladies assume expressions of glazed incomprehension. Only Dean Spanley seems alert and interested.

NARRATOR (V.O.): ...Indeed, the most significant fact I gleaned from the experience was, that with my eyes closed, the lecturer could have been a Welshman.

And then we are BACK with the Swami who says, concluding,

SWAMI PRASH: ...I should now be pleased to take any questions you might have.

And the Narrator nudges his father into wakefulness, a state he signals by saying, abruptly,

FISK: Where am I...?

The Swami smiles, a tolerant affair,

SWAMI PRASH: You are, my dear sir, in the ante-room of eternity with the rest of us sojourning souls.

And this remark brings Fisk entirely awake. He stares at the Swami, frowning. The Swami, having dealt with this matter, looks outward again and is rewarded by one of the ladies, urged on by the other, raising her hand,

SWAMI PRASH: Yes, Madam...?

1ST LADY: I was, eh, we were, that is, wondering if, eh, you could tell us about the souls of, well, animals...if they have them, that is...animals...

She looks at her companion to see if she has the enquiry right. The other lady nods, and adds,

2ND LADY: Pets, really. The souls of pets...

Wrather turns to look at them, his brows beetled in annoyance. Turns back.

WRATHER: The souls of pets. What next? The brains of budgerigars...?

Fisk, however, is still absorbing the Swami's previous answer.

FISK: Did he say, 'the anteroom of eternity'...?

Then Swami Prash proceeds,

SWAMI PRASH: That is a most interesting questions, mesdames, and I thank you for asking it...

And the Narrator, who has turned to look at the two ladies, as much to escape his father's query, as anything, notes that Spanley is leaning forward, his whole being focused on the man on the dais as he says,

SWAMI PRASH: It is generally supposed that the animal soul, if it is allowed such a faculty, must be of a different, and by inference, inferior, nature to the human soul. This is to mistake the nature of soul entirely. The soul is without qualification in this fashion. It is neither animal nor human.

The soul is that part of the Godhead, of All That Is, which expresses Itself in the physical world and animals possess them in exactly the same measure as do we...

And this brings a little flutter of excitement from the two ladies. The Narrator checks on them, but glances also at Spanley who has not moved or changed his expression. The Swami continues, ignoring Fisk who has begun to raise his hand like a child asking to go to the toilet.

SWAMI PRASH: ...This error leads to another, that for the human soul to be re-born in anything other than another human is by way of demotion on the ladder of life. Life, however, is not a ladder, but a wheel, and reversion through rebirth to other forms of consciousness is but part of the great karmic revolution in which we all participate in order to fulfil our purpose, which, simply put, is to become One with God and dwell in the Eternal Now.

At which point, Fisk says, unable to contain himself any longer,

FISK: What you said before, sir, about the anteroom of eternity...

Then from BEHIND him Spanley's VOICE, sharp with authority, cuts across him.

DEAN SPANLEY: Will you be so kind as to allow the Swami to continue his thought, sir...

And Fisk turns, shoots a glare at the Dean, then looks at the Narrator who returns it without encouragement.

FISK: Well, well...

And Swami Prash goes on in his cadenced way.

> **SWAMI PRASH:** ...However, although, all animals have their specific awareness of the God-head, and on this point all sages agree, the Dog is unique by virtue of the singular relationship it has with mankind...

And the two ladies look disappointed at this accolade, as the Swami goes on.

> **SWAMI PRASH:** ...Indeed, it is the view of those adepts who are permitted access to recall of previous existences, that their present incarnation was preceded directly by that of a dog...

And at this point, the ladies interject, almost plaintively,

> **LADIES:** What about cats...?

> **SWAMI PRASH:** Cats, Mesdames, offer a different paradigm. If it can be said that a man aspires to be the kind of person his dog believes him to be, the cat represents a calculated snub to human vanity and ego-centeredness. The dog amplifies, the cat diminishes, man's estimation of himself.

There is a short pause as the listeners absorb this into which Fisk complains, audibly,

> **FISK:** Poppycock...

DISSOLVE TO:

12 INT. ROOM - DAY

The lecture is over and the Swami is talking to Dean Spanley. The two ladies have gone and the Narrator is attempting to get his father to follow. Wrather stands with them, muttering,

WRATHER: Never trust a teetotaller or a man who wears elastic-sided boots, and if you ask me this fellow is guilty on both counts.

NARRATOR: Shall we go, Father...?

FISK: I want to ask him what he meant by quoting me without authority, dammit. And I shall, when that Spanley chap is done...the impertinence of the fellow, cutting me off when I was asking a perfectly valid question...

Just then the Dean moves off, and before the Narrator can restrain him, Fisk marches up to the Swami, saying,

FISK: Excuse my insistence, but I mean to know where you came by the expression, 'the anteroom of eternity...'

The Swami looks at the irate old man,

SWAMI PRASH: I have really no idea, sir. It came to me as I spoke, rising out of the ground of being in which we are all embedded. Does it have especial resonance for you, might I ask...?

FISK: Indeed it does. It's a coinage of my own as young Fisk here, who has heard me utter it many times, will attest.

SWAMI PRASH: Then I congratulate you, sir, for having established such a pregnant image in the etheric realm where it clearly has become incarnate. Else, how could I have found it, ready made, in my mouth?

Fisk has no answer to this and the Swami, seeing him so nonplussed, raises his palms, bows his head and LEAVES.

CUT TO:

13 EXT. MANSION - DAY

The Narrator, his father, now back in the wheelchair, on the gravel, Wrather taking his leave.

WRATHER: Well, I shall bid you gentlemen good day...

He produces a card, hands it to the Narrator.

WRATHER: I can be found here most mornings, and of an occasional evening...

The card gives his name and occupation: 'J.J. Wrather. Conveyancer.'

NARRATOR: What is 'conveyancing' exactly?

WRATHER: It's nothing 'exactly.' More of a service of facilitation. Assisting a thing to be moved between parties.

NARRATOR: So, you're a middle man.

WRATHER: Sometimes I'm in the middle. Sometimes I'm at either end...

Then to Fisk, extending his hand.

WRATHER: ...It's been a pleasure, sir.

FISK: Hmph... you're easily pleased, Mr Wrather, is all I can say...

And Wrather strides off, gets into his car, undisturbed by this last. The Narrator watches him go, then turns his father's chair in the direction of home.

NARRATOR: So you found the Swami's presentation entirely without interest I take it, apart from the plagiarism...

Starting to push him, as Wrather, with a roar and a toot of the horn goes past them, drawing another glare from Fisk. Then, as the car disappears down the drive,

FISK: Damned Colonials...

Then, as they proceed, he goes on.

FISK: ...The only thing that made sense in that whole damn farrago was what he said about dogs thinking you're better than you are...

NARRATOR: Canine flattery is a survival mechanism, according to Charles Darwin...

Which brings Fisk's head round to glare at him.

FISK: Then the man never had a dog, is all I can say.

And the Narrator, straight-faced, says,

NARRATOR: Didn't he have a Beagle at one time?

Drollery that is wasted on Fisk who faces front again, goes on in a kind of vexed mutter.

FISK: I had a dog once. Wag. One of the seven great dogs...at any given time you know, there are only seven. Did you know that...?

Glancing round at the Narrator who says, vaguely,

NARRATOR: No, can't say that I did...

FISK: Hrrmph. Neither did that Swami. Made me think he didn't know much about dogs...

They come to an intersection and the Narrator turns for home only to have Fisk countermand him, saying,

FISK: Let's go to my club, have a stiff one...

NARRATOR: I thought you never went there any more...?

FISK: That was in the past. This is the present, young Fisk. There's no time like the present. What was it the Swami called it...the Eternal Now...

And dutifully, the Narrator turns the chair and starts off.

14 EXT. CLUB - DAY

At the entrance, Fisk gets out of the chair, goes up the steps and through the swing doors while the Narrator entrusts the wheelchair to the Doorman.

15 INT. FOYER - DAY

Fisk has been met by the ATTENDANT at the desk who doesn't recognize him, even as Fisk says,

> **FISK:** How are you, Marriot...?

> **MARRIOT:** Oh, eh, very well, sir. And yourself...?

> **FISK:** Another day nearer the grave. How's that boy of yours, Tommy isn't it...?

> **MARRIOT:** Ah, yes, well, Tommy's dead, sir. In the war you know. The Boer War.

> **FISK:** Ah yes, the Boers. Lost one myself in that nonsense...

The Narrator has COME IN, stands looking around. Marriot, still trying to recall Fisk's name, says,

> **MARRIOT:** Haven't seen you in a while, sir...

> **FISK:** Haven't been here in years. Nothing's much changed though...

Looking from the entrance hall into the reading room where a regatta of newspapers billows from club chairs.

> **MARRIOT:** Would you like to sign in, sir?

FISK: Oh, yes...this is young Fisk. He's not a member, but I'll vouch for him...

And relieved at this clue, Marriot goes and opens the book.

MARRIOT: Of course, Mr Fisk, good to see you again, sir...

Fisk scrawls something on the page and he and the Narrator go into the reading room.

16 INT. READING ROOM - DAY

A high-ceilinged room with long windows letting in great slabs of light. They find a couple of chairs by one of the windows, settle down. Fisk looks around.

FISK: Hasn't changed much.

NARRATOR: Clubs aren't supposed to change, surely. Part of their appeal.

FISK: Hrmmph.

Looking around. He freezes, stares harder.

FISK: There's that chap again. Is he following us...?

The Narrator looks over to where Dean Spanley sits alone, a glass of some gleaming golden liquid in his hand, his nose poised above the rim. Fisk gets up.

NARRATOR: Where are you going?

FISK: Want to ask him what he thought of all that nonsense earlier...

And the Narrator gets up, follows him, a little hesitant to break in on the Dean's reverie. Fisk, however, marches straight up, causing Spanley to remove his attention from the glass and look inquiringly at the arrivals. There is a look in his eyes, a puzzlement far beyond the fact that he doesn't recognize them. It's the look of a man taken abruptly from some other region of mind. Seeing it, Fisk brusquely says,

> **FISK:** Fisk. Horatio Fisk...

> **DEAN SPANLEY:** Oh, Mr Fisk...

His voice vague. Fisk indicates the Narrator who stands behind him.

> **FISK:** This is young Fisk. Surprised we were to see you at the Nawab's...

And Spanley nods, remembering now.

> **DEAN SPANLEY:** Ah, yes...

> **FISK:** So, what did you make of all that mumble jumble...?

Spanley sets down his glass with an air of regret.

> **DEAN SPANLEY:** The beliefs of others are always of interest...

> **FISK:** Well, tell me this, then. Why don't they get in touch? Souls, I mean. Never a word from beyond the grave. You'd think one of them would have given a shout...hmmph...

Spanley considers this a moment, then

> **DEAN SPANLEY:** If the Swami is to be believed, they are all too busy being who they've become...

Fisk grunts, unconvinced, but the Narrator is taken by this explanation, and is about to ask Spanley a question, when his father goes on, harking back,

> **FISK:** And what about him pinching my line?

> **DEAN SPANLEY:** What 'line' was that?

> **FISK:** 'The anteroom of eternity.'

And Spanley remembers now, and his own interjection.

> **DEAN SPANLEY:** I had rather thought it a common usage...

> **FISK:** Nothing of the sort. Out of my own head that came.

> **DEAN SPANLEY:** Indeed.

> **FISK:** Felt like having your pocket picked. What's that you're drinking...?

> **DEAN SPANLEY:** It is a Tokay. An Imperial Tokay...

> **FISK:** Looks a bit syrupy for my taste. Well, then, we'll leave you to it...

And as abruptly as he arrived, Fisk marches off. The Narrator, embarrassed by the whole business, says,

> **NARRATOR:** You must excuse my father. He can be rather impulsive...

> **DEAN SPANLEY:** Not at all...

> **NARRATOR:** So, am I to understand you give some credence to these matters, Dean?

Spanley considers this in his judicious manner for a moment.

DEAN SPANLEY: Only the closed mind is certain, sir.

And with that, he raises his glass again in a kind of salutation that is also a closure, and the Narrator, impressed, intrigued, nods.

NARRATOR: I agree... Good day, sir...

Taking his leave, and joins his father back at their table. Sits down opposite him.

FISK: Rum chap, Spanley...

NARRATOR: Do you know him well enough to have such an opinion?

FISK: One can tell. Not quite sound. Dabbling in Eastern religion. Drinking muck like that...

Marriot appears.

MARRIOT: Can I bring you gentlemen a drink?

FISK: I'll have a brandy soda, with the emphasis on the brandy...

NARRATOR: I'll have a glass of the Tokay. The Imperial...

And he nods towards Spanley who has recommenced his veneration of the liquid in his glass.

MARRIOT: I'm afraid that's not possible, sir. The Tokay is private stock. The Dean keeps a bottle for his personal use... Very hard to come by, I believe...

FISK: Damned unsociable of him. Told you the fellow wasn't sound.

NARRATOR: I'll have a brandy soda, in the inverse ratio...

MARRIOT: Very good, sir. And if I may say, so Mr Fisk, I'm most sorry to hear of your loss...

Fisk stares at him, uncomprehending, and Marriot sees it.

MARRIOT: Your son, sir. In the War...

FISK: Wasn't my loss. He's the one got killed...

Nonplussed, Marriot withdraws. The Narrator stares at his father, exasperated, embarrassed.

NARRATOR: That was, even for you, Father, a singularly callous remark.

Fisk stares at him, quite unperturbed.

FISK: Nothing of the sort. Here we sit about to be served brandy and sodas. What's our loss compared to your brother's?

And the Narrator can't bring himself to argue further. He looks away and SEES Spanley finishing his Tokay with a last reverential sip. Then he rises, nodding to them as he passes, on his way out.

CUT TO:

17 EXT. STREET - DAY

The Narrator pushing Fisk Sr along.

NARRATOR (V.O.): Walking home, listening to my father assert a variety of things in tones of un-brookable authority...

FISK: ...Women with the vote would be like a cow with a gun... contrary to nature.

NARRATOR (V.O.): ...Dean Spanley's words returned to me with renewed force...

FISK: ...That damned war your brother went to will be the last for a while, mark my words, which is more than he did...

NARRATOR (V.O.): 'Only the closed mind is certain.'

17A INT. STUDY - DAY

The Narrator is reading to his father who is drifting off under the quilt of words.

NARRATOR: 'It may well be supposed that this turn of events came as a most disagreeable surprise to Mr Chuttleworth, accustomed as he was to having his every whim catered for...

We HEAR as the reading proceeds in DUMBSHOW,

NARRATOR (V.O.): I confess I had, until that moment, always supposed certainty to be rather a good thing. Like money in the bank, or a membership at Lords...

He sees his father has nodded off, puts down the book.

NARRATOR (V.O.): ...But something in the day's events had occasioned in me a certain disquiet, a sense that...

He closes the book, stands up and, aloud to his sleeping parent,

NARRATOR: ...There may be more in heaven and earth than is dreamt of in your philosophy, Horatio...

And at the use of his name, Fisk twitches, still in his sleep and says something, a mere mumble that sounds like 'here boy,' or 'Herbert' or 'Harriston' and the Narrator goes out.

17B INT. LIBRARY - DAY

The Narrator walking through the library. He stops, look at the wall where a faint rectangular outline shows that a painting once hung there. It's evident this gap means something to the Narrator although he only pauses a moment, then walks on.

17C INT. KITCHEN - DAY

The Narrator looks in to find Mrs Brimley sitting in a chair busy over a needlework hoop. We have the impression that she might have been saying something to the empty chair opposite. She looks round at the intrusion.

NARRATOR: Ah, Mrs Brimley...I'm going out for a walk. He's nodded off. I'll be back for dinner...

MRS BRIMLEY: Very good, Mr Henslowe. It's hot pot again. Won't have nothing else on a Thursday...

NARRATOR: He's a creature of habit, Mrs Brimley...

She sniffs.

> **MRS BRIMLEY:** Don't I know it...dinner will be at
> six-thirty.
> **NARRATOR:** I won't be late...

*And he leaves her. She settles back into her chair and to the
other chair says,*

> **MRS BRIMLEY:** Must have made five hundred of
> those hot pots if I've made one.

CUT TO:

21 EXT. CATHEDRAL GROUNDS -
LATE AFTERNOON

*The foliage of a tree fills the screen. In its branches a CAT
crouches. FROM OFF-CAMERA a GROWL is heard, causing
the cat to hiss down at the source. We HEAR:*

> **NARRATOR (V.O.):** I've heard it said that one
> encounter is a happenstance, two a coincidence,
> and three, a significance...

*And the SHOT WIDENS and we see that the tree is in the
grounds of the cathedral and that Dean Spanley is standing
beneath it, looking up. There is no sign of any dog to explain
the growling.*

*BEHIND Spanley, on the other side of the railings, we can see
the Narrator and HEAR:*

> **NARRATOR (V.O.):** ...Be that as it may, that
> evening I found myself, for the third time, in the
> presence of Dean Spanley, a man who, until that
> day, I did not know existed...

And the Narrator calls out.

NARRATOR: Is it stuck up there?

The Dean looks round, then back up the tree.

DEAN SPANLEY: It rather appears so...they never seem to think of that when they go up, which I consider a serious reflection on their intelligence.

NARRATOR: Probably chased by a dog.

DEAN SPANLEY: Humph...

And he looks as if he is ready to walk away.

NARRATOR: Dean... Dean Spanley....?

Spanley looks round.

NARRATOR: ...Excuse me, but we met earlier today. At your club. I was introduced to you by my father... Mr Fisk...

Spanley comes over, slowly, out of politeness we feel.

DEAN SPANLEY: Ah, yes, Mr Fisk...

NARRATOR: And of course we met earlier at the Nawab's...

Spanley stares at him, and the Narrator, sensing his time is running out, says,

NARRATOR: It made me most eager to hear your further views on the subject of re-incarnation...

DEAN SPANLEY: I assure you, sir, I have no especial knowledge on the matter...

NARRATOR: Compared to my own, I'm sure yours is encyclopaedic... I wondered if you might have dinner with me one evening...

Spanley doesn't look too enthusiastic, indeed a little taken aback.

DEAN SPANLEY: I'm afraid my schedule is such that, that would be rather difficult.

NARRATOR: I would not presume upon so short an acquaintance were it not for the remarkable coincidence of having recently come into possession of a bottle of Tokay... an Imperial Tokay...

And he sees he has hit the right note from the Dean's immediate interest.

DEAN SPANLEY: An Imperial Tokay...?

NARRATOR: Yes...

DEAN SPANLEY: One must be on one's guard against the common or garden variety...what year?

Which takes the Narrator unexpectedly but he continues, in for a pound, now.

NARRATOR: An '89, I believe...

And Spanley's face widens in an expression in which disbelief and awe are mingled.

DEAN SPANLEY: An '89, you say...?

NARRATOR: Was...is...that a good year?

DEAN SPANLEY: Most excellent. How did you ever come by such a treasure? You must be very well connected, Mr... Mr...?

NARRATOR: Fisk, Henslowe Fisk...sir.

DEAN SPANLEY: Yes. Well... perhaps I might manage next Thursday, if that would be convenient...?

NARRATOR: Most convenient, sir... Shall we say, seven o'clock?

And he produces a card, hands it through the railings. Spanley takes it, looks at it. Puts it in his pocket.

DEAN SPANLEY: Very well... until then... an '89... most excellent...

And he walks off.

FROM the tree there comes a MEOW. The Narrator looks up into the tree.

NARRATOR: I should not call it a lie, puss.
A premature truth, perhaps, but nothing worse,
I'm sure...

But the cat is not so sure, and says so.

CUT TO:

21A EXT. STREET - EVENING

The Narrator is seen coming along the street and going into a wine merchants, where, through the window, we see him ask and be disappointed in DUMBSHOW.

CUT TO:

21B INT. WINE MERCHANT'S - EVENING

Another wine shop, just closing as the Narrator enters and, where once again, we see him fail to find what he needs. We HEAR:

PROPRIETOR (V.O.): Haven't seen a bottle of the Imperial in...well, don't think I've ever seen one, tell you the truth, sir...

21C EXT. STREET - NIGHT

The Narrator walking home. We HEAR:

NARRATOR (V.O.): It had not occurred to me when I made my overture to the Dean that procuring his favourite tipple would prove such a challenge.

DISSOLVE TO:

23 INT. ANOTHER WINE MERCHANT - DAY

The PROPRIETOR of the shop is explaining to the Narrator:

PROPRIETOR: Very hard to come by an Imperial Tokay, sir. There are what you might call commercial counterfeits, but the real thing, well, that's an altogether different story. It's made solely for the Hapsburg monarchy, you see. Takes a Royal Decree to have one uncorked. You'd need to know somebody who had such connections...

NARRATOR: Well, say King Edward came to you and said, 'Can you find me a bottle or two of Tokay,' what would you tell him?

PROPRIETOR: I would suggest, most respectfully, that he uses his family connections to effect the conveyancing. He'd have a lot more chance of success than I would...

NARRATOR: I see...conveyancing, you say...

As the thought occurs to him. He LEAVES the shop searching a waistcoat pocket, and brings out Wrather's card, looks at it.

NARRATOR: Well, let's see just how much of a conveyancer you are, Mr Wrather...

CUT TO:

24 INT. BILLIARD ROOM - DAY

Wrather and the Narrator are in a large room, the centre of which holds a billiard table on which Wrather is setting up the balls in a fashion that requires them all be potted one after the other without a miss. The rest of the room is given over to a miscellany of items: pieces of statuary, paintings, a tuba, stuffed animals, clocks, an armoire, and a birdcage holding a PARROT that speaks the word 'Help!' in a rising, distinctly antipodean accent.

The Narrator has just experienced this performance and stares alarmed at Wrather who's just finished setting up his solitaire. He nods at the Narrator's expression, coming round to put a cloth over the cage.

WRATHER: Belonged to my Aunt Molly. Nervous type, but too polite to scream...

NARRATOR: I see...is that all it can say?

WRATHER: 'Fraid so. Limits its appeal to some. You wouldn't be interested...?

NARRATOR: It admiringly expresses a condition I am familiar with, but I think not...

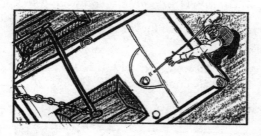

Wrather doesn't look too disappointed, lines up his first shot, explaining,

WRATHER: The point of the exercise is to drop every ball without a miss. Care to wager a small sum...?

NARRATOR: I have the feeling you are more than capable of such a feat...

As Wrather begins. After enough balls have gone down to substantiate this assessment, Wrather says, still playing,

WRATHER: So, you want to acquire a bottle of an '89 Tokay...

NARRATOR: An Imperial...

WRATHER: Just so. This an adventure of the romantic sort you're embarking on?

NARRATOR: No, nothing of that sort.

WRATHER: It's said the fair sex responds avidly to Tokay...loosens the morals and with it the corsets.

NARRATOR: I can assure you...

WRATHER: I'm in no need of assurance. Man of the world, me. How high are you willing to go...?

NARRATOR: Well, whatever it costs, I dare say. Within reason...

WRATHER: Ah well, the 'within reason' part is the rub. Not easily come by, an '89 Tokay.

NARRATOR: So I have gathered...

Wrather sinks two more balls. Then,

WRATHER: So, if it's not a lady, who is it you're trying to impress...?

The Narrator hesitates, and Wrather holds up a palm.

WRATHER: ...No need to divulge anything you'd rather not...

NARRATOR: I have invited Dean Spanley to have dinner with me...

Wrather hesitates on his next shot, casts his mind back, fishes out the reference.

WRATHER: The Dean? This have something to do with that reincarnation business...?

NARRATOR: Not at all. I met him at my father's club. Tokay is his favourite wine... that's all...and he seems an interesting sort...

Wrather raises his eyebrows.

WRATHER: Well, he'll have to be damned interesting to justify splashing out on this stuff... An '89, you say. You certainly know your Tokay, Young Fisk...

He sinks a ball for emphasis, then, putting up his cue,

WRATHER: ...Well, let's see what we have lying around...

CUT TO:

24A EXT. BACK AREA - DAY

Wrather and the Narrator come out of the back door, make their way across considerable grounds towards a set of low stone structures.

WRATHER: So what's your line, then...?

NARRATOR: Bookseller...antiquarian...

WRATHER: Is there money in it?

The Narrator looks a little sniffy at this, but says,

NARRATOR: There is modest remuneration. The real reward is in the books themselves.

Wrather unlocks the door to one of the vaults. The Narrator looks back at the house.

NARRATOR: ...I think there must be rather more in conveyancing...

As Wrather gets the door open. He looks back at the house, then at the tone in the Narrator's voice.

WRATHER: Not all mine. I'm just a ground floor tenant...

And goes into the vault, the Narrator following him.

24B INT. VAULT - DAY

The vault, which is of considerable extent, is a reprise of the billiard room inasmuch as it contains a very considerable number of items, similarly eclectic: a harpsichord, a ship's figurehead, stone columns, large canvases, as well as boxes of dishes, tools, books and in places crates of wine.

The Narrator stands looking around in bewilderment, as Wrather goes rummaging.

NARRATOR: How on earth do you come by so much...stuff...?

WRATHER: Auntie Molly was a hoarder. Caught it from her, I shouldn't wonder...

NARRATOR: But what do you do with it?

WRATHER: Oh, you never know when somebody will want something you just happen to have...

NARRATOR: Sounds rather, well, hit or miss.

WRATHER: ...Such as a bottle of Imperial Tokay...

Bringing the very item out of an otherwise empty crate. The Narrator stares at this feat of legerdemain in astonishment. Comes over to examine the bottle.

NARRATOR: Well, I declare myself amazed.

Wrather dusts it off.

WRATHER: Not an '89, I'm afraid. '91...will that do...?

NARRATOR: Well, I suppose it will have to. I'll say I was promised an '89, but the man was mistaken...I know that's taking a somewhat elastic view of the truth...how much is it...?

WRATHER: Five guineas to you.

NARRATOR: Five guineas...I say, that's rather steep...

His tone conveying his opinion of this estimate.

WRATHER: These little things are sent to try us, as the man said of the Pygmy judge...

And the Narrator brings out his purse.

Above Producers Alan Harris (left) and Matthew Metcalfe.

Left Director Toa Fraser with his rugby ball, which provided entertainment and exercise for the cast.

Below Writer Alan Sharp discusses putting words on to the screen.

Above Some of the extras, including MCC members recommended by Peter O'Toole, gather for a group portrait after filming at the Nawab's mansion.

Left Bryan Brown and Matthew Metcalfe look forward to filming in New Zealand.

Right The camera gets in close on Jeremy Northam.

Left One of several genuine vintage cars that were hired to give the film authenticity.

Above Toa Fraser and Cinematographer Leon Narbey run through a scene.

Right Often the director would only have to whisper a single word to Peter O'Toole in order to get the perfect take.

Above The Tokay is prepared and lit for the perfect "sniff".

Below Jeremy Northam learns his lines.

Left Leon Narbey sets up a shot. With the production moved to New Zealand, a different colour palette and set-up would help create the world of the Dean's memories.

Right The shepherd (played by Bruce Hopkins) receives some special make-up attention to his teeth.

Below The two dog actors rehearse a scene.

Above The four principal actors share notes during the climactic scene 48.

Left What the director saw (in his monitor).

Right Xavier Horan (Harrington Fisk) practices falling off his horse.

Above The crew prepare to capture Peter O'Toole's performance.

Right Fake snow is used to create the perfect English winter.

Below The dogs are shown how to relax in the New Zealand shade.

Above Sam Neill and Bryan Brown: Haven't we met before?

Right Counting down the days until Christmas.

24C EXT. FISK HOUSE - GARDEN - DAY

The Narrator is with his father who is not taking the news of a change in his schedule at all well.

FISK: ...Thursday...!? Are there not six other perfectly adequate days, each equipped with portions of time suitable for such activities?. Why must the day of my outing be given over to something other...?

NARRATOR: Thursday is the only day the Dean is free.

FISK: Poppycock. Deans have dinner every evening.

NARRATOR: Prior engagements...

FISK: Is my Thursday not a prior engagement, Young Fisk...? Why should not Spanley rearrange his schedule rather than myself...?

Fisk stares at him, irate, and suddenly suspicious.

FISK: What is all this about? You're not thinking of getting married, I hope.

And the Narrator is totally taken aback by this.

NARRATOR: Married...certainly not.

FISK: Good... If I had it to do over again...

He shakes his head vigorously. The Narrator, offended, says, coldly,

NARRATOR: Am I to understand that you regret marrying Mother...?

FISK: Fine woman, Alice, very good in the garden. No, it's the children. Hostages to fortune, is what they are. But, there's no point to regretting things that have gone to the trouble of happening...

NARRATOR: Is that your reason for not mourning Harrington?

Fisk flashes him a look of affront.

FISK: I warned your brother that war would be bad for his health. But no, he knew better, the young fool, went off in his prime, last we saw of him...

And he pauses for a moment, then shakes his head almost dismissively.

FISK: Anyway, his mother mourned him enough for both of us...

NARRATOR: Perhaps if you had shared that burden with her, she might not have found her grief so unsupportable.

And this causes Fisk to freeze in a posture of outrage and he goes to sit in his chair, his back to the Narrator.

FISK: I have nothing more to say on this subject. Please never raise it with me again. Close the door on your way out...

And after a moment in which we can see the Narrator regretting his remark, he turns and leaves.

CUT TO:

27 INT. KITCHEN - EVENING

The Narrator is standing looking at several PHOTOGRAPHS on the mantel. One is of two boys, stood by a rowboat with a wide expanse of water behind them. Mrs Brimley is at the table, preparing food.

NARRATOR: Do you miss Albert, Mrs Brimley...?

Which surprises her.

MRS BRIMLEY: Miss him? Well, he weren't hard to miss, Albert. Kept himself to himself, sat in that chair night after night, never said a word. Just nodded, sociable-like, or spat in the fire now'n again. That was Albert's one bad habit. I talk to the chair sometimes and it's just like old times. 'Cept the chair don't spit...

And then after this little riffle of talk, she looks at him again.

MRS BRIMLEY: Thinking 'bout your brother and your mum, are you...?

The Narrator stands a moment, then nods.

NARRATOR: I could just wish that my father could bring himself to...

And he makes a gesture, uncertain, incomplete.

MRS BRIMLEY: Mr Fisk never was a-one for showing much. Why, I remember that night, up on the lake, when you and young Harry went out in that cockleshell of a boat...

Young Fisk clearly doesn't want to be reminded.

NARRATOR: Yes, yes, not his finest hour. Well, I'll let you get on, Mrs Brimley. Good night...

And he goes out, and she looks after him a moment, a shrewd light in her eyes, says,

MRS BRIMLEY: And don't you worry about Thursday, Mr Henslowe. I'll feed him the hot pot and he'll be right as rain. You just enjoy yourself with your friend...

DISSOLVE TO:

27A EXT. BUILDING DAY/NIGHT

A SHOT establishing the façade of the Narrator's dwelling, arcing through a day/night time span while we HEAR:

NARRATOR (V.O.): But as the event drew closer, I found my enthusiasm for it waning, for in truth the whim that prompted me to extend the invitation had lost its piquancy and the sobering cost of Wrather's Tokay played its part in making the whole venture seem somewhat dubious...

CUT TO:

27B INT. APARTMENT - DAY

The Narrator's apartment shows signs of his occupancy, being home to a large collection of serious looking books. The place, otherwise, is sparsely furnished, in the manner of a bachelor.

The single most noticeable feature of the somewhat austere interior is a portrait of a young man in the uniform of a prestigious regiment, staring out with enthusiasm and certainty from above the fireplace. The CAMERA examines all this and finally finds, in the dining room where a table has been set for two, a decanter of a lustrous, honey-coloured liquid, and we HEAR:

NARRATOR (V.O.): I'm afraid I was misinformed of the vintage. It transpires that the '89 was not in fact available...this is a '91...I hope that is not too much of a disappointment.

And the SHOT WIDENS to find Spanley staring at the decanter and the emptied bottle beside it.

DEAN SPANLEY: Not at all, one would have to have a most jaded palate indeed if the prospect of a '91 Kleverheld-Manschliess were a disappointment.

He examines the bottle, checking the sediment in the bottom, and then the decanter.

DEAN SPANLEY: ...And properly decanted, no trace of sediment, well done...

He puts the bottle back, and returns his loving gaze to the wine.

DEAN SPANLEY: ...To think that such wine was once only opened by decree of a Hapsburg, and now, through the vicissitudes of history we lesser beings may command such an audience...

And we see the Dean through the lens of the decanter, an aperture that imports a certain distortion to his features and emphasizes a rapt dog-like intensity of focus. We HEAR the Narrator's voice and during his words DISSOLVE THROUGH TO the table and the two of them sitting there, the lunch over, and the decanter between them.

NARRATOR (V.O.): I must admit my first taste of the Tokay was not an illuminating one...

And we see him pour a glass for himself and the Dean, who again has that almost transfixed expression of anticipation.

NARRATOR (V.O.): ...Indeed, my father's dismissal of it as being too syrupy seemed remarkably close to the mark...

The Dean is savouring the bouquet, eyes half closed, entirely focused in his nose.

NARRATOR (V.O.): ...However, in Dean Spanley, its champion was to hand...

As Spanley ventures his first sip and says, after a moment of reverential silence,

DEAN SPANLEY: Ah, Mr Fisk...

And looks gratefully across his glass at his host.

DEAN SPANLEY: ...Tokay is unique among wines in as much as the aroma is more significant than the flavour. We humans are, alas, under-equipped to enjoy the distinction. Indeed, for us, it is the pursuit of the ineffable by the inadequate...

He breathes it in again, then,

DEAN SPANLEY: ...At such moments, one could wish to posses the olfactory powers of the canine...

For a moment, they sit, the Narrator taking reluctant sips, while the Dean drinks more enthusiastically, and suddenly, in a totally different train of thought, says,

DEAN SPANLEY: It has often occurred to me that to pull a dog away from a lamp post is akin to seizing a scholar in the British Museum by the scruff of his neck and dragging him away from his studies...

The Narrator, a little caught out by this, can only nod. Spanley drinks some more, again with that rapt air, draining his glass with evident relish.

FROM OUTSIDE comes the sound of brakes being heavily applied and the blare of a horn. Spanley pays the interruption not the slightest mind, concentrating on his glass as the Narrator refills it, saying,

NARRATOR: One of those motor machines. Dreadful things, don't you think?

Spanley can only stare at the Tokay as it spills into his glass. Then when the Narrator has withdrawn the decanter, he says, with an attempt at consecutive thought,

DEAN SPANLEY: Indeed. It must be clear to anyone with the slightest perception that the invention of the internal, one might even say 'infernal' combustion engine will prove to be a terrible catastrophe for the species...

And he takes another drink, and goes on, a distant look in his eyes.

DEAN SPANLEY: ...And have you noticed that motor cars are exactly the right height for them to take refuge under...

And the Narrator stares at him, baffled.

NARRATOR: I beg your pardon...?

DEAN SPANLEY: Cats, the way they get under motor cars and can't be got at...unless, of course, you are a very small dog...

NARRATOR: Yes, I see, now you mention it...

Not knowing what the Dean is talking about, and toying with his glass, at a loss to contribute anything more substantial to this observation. After a moment, Spanley continues in the same vein.

DEAN SPANLEY: The trouble with cats is they have no idea of the rules... When one chases them, they invariably hide or climb trees...or perform that preposterous inflation they're so fond of, raising their hair on end...

He drinks again as the Narrator tries to keep up. Then,

DEAN SPANLEY: One should never be fooled by this ruse...

NARRATOR: I beg your pardon...?

Said in a tone of having missed something. Spanley looks up at him, frowning.

DEAN SPANLEY: Well, perhaps when I was very young I was taken in by it once or twice, but once I learned what devious and subversive creatures they are...

And he goes back to his glass, inhaling, sipping as the Narrator tries to keep the conversation going, not quite sure of its direction but piqued now by some element previously missing.

NARRATOR: So you are inclined to agree with the Swami about them. Cats, and how they diminish man's estimation of himself...

DEAN SPANLEY: Oh, indeed. They have no awe of the Masters...none at all...

Which causes the Narrator to check that he is hearing correctly, asking,

NARRATOR: The 'Masters'...?

Spanley nods, looks over the rim of his glass, a faraway expression in his eyes as if something wonderful had been recalled to him.

DEAN SPANLEY: Yes... How one loved to be in their company. How one wanted to please them, if only by obedience...

Then, suddenly focusing on the Narrator, he says,

DEAN SPANLEY: ...Let me give you one piece of advice. When a door is opened, always take that opportunity to leave the room. There's nothing so annoying to the Master as a dog whining and scratching to get out...

And then a little flash of panic crosses Spanley's face, as if he'd just heard himself and didn't know what he was talking about.

The Narrator, seeing the Dean's confusion, proffers the decanter.

Spanley stares at it, distracted, then shakes his head in an over-vigorous way.

DEAN SPANLEY: No, thank you. Two glasses are my limit. One must know one's limits... otherwise, there's no knowing where things will end up...

And he shakes his head again, as if ridding himself of disturbing thoughts.

CUT TO:

29 INT. WRATHER'S HOUSE - BILLIARD ROOM - DAY

Wrather is at his game while the Narrator paces around the table, saying,

NARRATOR: I didn't know what to think. There he was giving me advice about going out of the room any time the door was opened and how dragging a dog away from a lamppost was like pulling a scholar out of the British Museum by the scruff of his neck...it was as if his mind had slipped a cog...

WRATHER: Went barking mad, you mean...?

NARRATOR: No, he was perfectly rational...if you can call remembering when you were a dog 'rational'.

WRATHER: How much had he had of the Tokay?

NARRATOR: Two glasses...

WRATHER: Not exactly a snootful...sure it wasn't you who was snockered...?

The Narrator shakes his head, meeting Wrather's sceptical gaze, saying helplessly,

NARRATOR: You would have had to have been there...

And the Narrator waits for the pending ridicule. Wrather, however, goes back to the table, saying, as he lines up a shot, over the cue,

WRATHER: Mind you, I do recall seeing his face when the Swami was talking about dogs and all that malarkey, and, he... well, he had that look...

NARRATOR: What look?

WRATHER: You know, the way they look when you're going to throw a stick for them to fetch...

The Narrator checks to see if Wrather really believes this, but his head is down as he plays the last shot. Then he looks up when it goes in. The Narrator, almost plaintively, asks,

NARRATOR: So you think... What do you think?

WRATHER: I think getting Deans tiddly so they can pretend to remember being dogs is as harmless a way to pass the time as any...

NARRATOR: He was not, as you put it 'tiddly'... more like an altered state of mind...

WRATHER: If being tiddly isn't an altered state, I don't know what is...

NARRATOR: It was the Tokay. He had two glasses of claret at dinner which left him sober as a... a Dean. But when he got to the Tokay, even just inhaling it, he was, well, that's when he was transported...to the other place...

Wrather looks at him,

WRATHER: And you want him to go there again, that it...?

The Narrator looks at him, nods,

NARRATOR: Can you get another bottle?

Wrather stares at him.

WRATHER: The old devil went through a whole bottle?

NARRATOR: No. But after he was gone, I, well, I experimented...to see if I could... Well, to see what effect it would have...

WRATHER: And...?

NARRATOR: If dogs have hangovers, I may well have been one...

Wrather pots another ball, the Narrator looks on, then,

NARRATOR: Well, can you...?

WRATHER: I've no doubt that for a price one will come to hand.

NARRATOR: And can you have it for next Thursday...?

CUT TO:

30 EXT. PARK - MORNING

*The Narrator is pushing Fisk in his wheelchair. A UNIFORMED
ENSEMBLE is playing on a nearby bandstand, the brassy,
melancholy music drifting over the privet hedges. Fisk is going
on in a querulous tone.*

FISK: So this is to become a regular feature
then...

NARRATOR: The Dean has a fund of knowledge
I find quite fascinating...

FISK: But only on a Thursday...

*At that moment a BOY of around 7 years comes around the
hedge, ignoring the calls of a Young Woman still out of sight.
As the Boy passes close, Fisk sticks out a foot and trips him,*

*sending him sprawling into the grass. It is so totally
unexpected that the Narrator can only stare in amazement,
while the Boy, spread out on the ground and stunned, lies
where he fell.*

*The YOUNG WOMAN who has been calling the Boy's name
comes round a hedge, and seeing her charge full length on the
ground, hurries toward him, already scolding the child.
Fisk turns round, saying,*

> **FISK:** Push on, let's get away from this music...
> can't stand all that brassy farting...

*But the Narrator has gone to lift up the Boy as the Young
Woman arrives. The Boy is crying now from a scrape on his
knee, and he points at Fisk,*

> **BOY:** That man tripped me up...

> **YOUNG WOMAN:** Don't be ridiculous...

And she looks apologetically at the Narrator.

> **YOUNG WOMAN:** He's given to imaginings...

*As Fisk starts to wheel himself off. Embarrassed, nonplussed,
the Narrator can only nod, and leaves the Young Woman with
her charge, to catch up with Fisk. He takes the wheelchair
handles and pushes until they are out of earshot, then,*

NARRATOR: That was quite unwarranted, Father, whatever possessed you to do such a thing...?

Fisk is unrepentant.

NARRATOR: No business running off like that when he was being summoned.

NARRATOR: You speak as if you were never a child yourself.

FISK: Indeed I was, and damned glad when it was over. Too much is made of childhood, to my mind. Golden days of fun and innocence. Poppycock. The most miserable I've been was as a child...

NARRATOR: Is that why you tripped him up, to teach him childhood isn't a happy time...?

And Fisk suddenly applies the brakes, stopping forward motion. Gets up, eyes aglitter.

FISK: Do not presume to judge me, Young Fisk...

NARRATOR: I think I should first have to understand you, Father, and I confess, I do not...

And after a moment of mutual staring, Fisk turns and strides off. The Narrator watches him go, and we see the little gesture again, the finger run around a too-tight collar before he turns and pushes the empty wheelchair in the opposite direction.

DISSOLVE TO:

31 INT. DINING ROOM - NIGHT

The Narrator and Spanley are at the table, the decanted Tokay in front of them, and by its level a fair amount has already gone down. Spanley has on his face that glaze of distracted satisfaction, as he accepts another pour from the golden goblet, raising it appreciatively to the light.

DEAN SPANLEY: What lambency of hue, what colour...it reminds me of the way the light looked when the Master came home...

Then as the Narrator, engrossed by this, overfills the glass, the train of thought is broken and he says, with asperity,

DEAN SPANLEY: Never to the brim...

DEAN SPANLEY: You must always leave room for the aroma...

NARRATOR: *The aroma, of course...you were saying...about the Master, when he came home...*

DEAN SPANLEY: Ah yes. The Master. He would go away for very long times. Other people were kind, but it was not the same...

NARRATOR: So what did you do?

DEAN SPANLEY: Why wait, of course. Until I knew he was back coming home...

NARRATOR: You knew when he was returning...?

DEAN SPANLEY: Oh yes...

NARRATOR: Ah, how, if I might ask?

DEAN SPANLEY: Well, because before he was not coming home, and then he was. That was the difference, plain and simple.

NARRATOR: Yes, I see...

Not seeing. Spanley nods judiciously over another sip, then,

DEAN SPANLEY: It's true, seeing is part of it... the proximity of the Master does affect the light...

NARRATOR: It grows... brighter?

DEAN SPANLEY: No, not brighter. Louder, perhaps.

NARRATOR: The light grows louder...?

DEAN SPANLEY: Certainly there is more of it. I can remember waiting when it was the day he was to return and all the day the light became stronger until one was quite dazzled...

He stops, as baffled as the Narrator who waits, agog. Finally Spanley says, his powers of explanation exhausted,

DEAN SPANLEY: ...I only know that when he finally came, I was so excited, I had several brandies to calm myself.

And this is too much for the Narrator who says, forgetting himself,

> **NARRATOR:** But dogs, surely, do not drink brandy...?

> **DEAN SPANLEY:** No more they do. I achieved the effect by running round in very small circles... drives the blood to the head in a most exhilarating fashion...

And we see at that moment a FLASH CUT of a young Welsh Spaniel doing that very thing, the briefest of cuts so that we do not have for it a POV, just the image, almost subliminal before we are BACK with the Dean saying, fondly,

CORKSCREW CRANE DOWN

> **DEAN SPANLEY:** Then I would sit down and have a good scratch.

And another FLASH CUT then BACK to the Narrator who, caught up in it all, goes on to say, as if it were the most normal thing in the world.

> **NARRATOR:** Were you much bothered by fleas?

Spanley, who has his Tokay to his nose looks over the rim, and the Narrator, suddenly fearful of having burst the bubble, says, hurriedly,

NARRATOR: When I say 'bothered', I don't mean to imply...

Only for Spanley to interrupt with,

DEAN SPANLEY: ...Oh, there is nothing wrong with a flea or two. They serve admirably to get one started on one's grooming...

And as we get another CUT to the Spaniel thus engaged, we HEAR:

NARRATOR (V.O.): It was at that moment, I realized I must obtain corroboration of these extraordinary reminiscences or else I should forever doubt my own witness...

And we see him glance at his brother's portrait in a kind of imploration before we come BACK to Spanley, concluding his description.

DEAN SPANLEY: ...Indeed, I doubt if one can be a dog and not have fleas...

CUT TO:

32 INT. WRATHER'S HOUSE - BILLIARD ROOM - DAY

The Narrator is pacing up and down as Wrather positions the balls for his game of solitaire. He looks up,

WRATHER: You don't think the Dean is having you on, do you?

The Narrator stops pacing, stares at him, incredulous.

NARRATOR: What do you mean, 'having me on'...?

WRATHER: Well, that he's spotted you for the gullible sort and also that you're a good source for his favourite drink.

NARRATOR: Nonsense. Why would he assume pretending to have been a dog would not bring forth disbelief and ridicule rather than repeated invitations to dinner...?

WRATHER: Well, he saw you at the Nawab's listening to all the nonsense about incarnation and dogs, and decided you believed in that sort of thing...

And he starts to pot the balls as the Narrator comes in with,

NARRATOR: No, I cannot believe that. It would be wholly unlike someone of his gravitas...

WRATHER: Gravitas? Telling you about running round in circles to get the effect of whisky and soda...?

NARRATOR: ...Brandy and soda...

WRATHER: ...And how fleas are good for grooming, and you talk about gravitas...?

NARRATOR: I tell you, he doesn't know when he is saying these things, and when he isn't...

WRATHER: I should have to see it for myself before I'd believe it...

And at that moment there comes a KNOCK at the door. Wrather pauses, puts down his cue, as it is repeated in a specific pattern.

WRATHER: Excuse me...a delivery...

And he goes OUT.

The Narrator stands in the midst of a decision. Almost absently he raises the cloth on the cage and is greeted by the rising crescendo of imploration from the parrot. He hastily re-covers the cage.

Wrather COMES BACK, carrying with some difficulty a stuffed warthog which he puts down and, breathing heavily, sits on.

WRATHER: Been frightening Molly, then?

NARRATOR: No, I mean, I just lifted the cover...
WRATHER: Does her good to sound off now and again...otherwise all those 'helps' build up inside her.

The Narrator stares at the warthog. Wrather notices, nods,

WRATHER: Ugly bugger. Can't for the life of me see why you'd have one stuffed. Now, about this Tokay. Harder than hobby horses' droppings to

come by, and ruinously expensive, as you
know...so how about if I can round one up,
you let me sit in on the séance...?

And seeing the Narrator's expression,

WRATHER: ...Or whatever it is goes on.

NARRATOR: It's a parting of the veil between one
life and another...

Wrather nods at this extravagant expression.

WRATHER: Right. At the veil parting...

*The Narrator stares at him a moment, then, with some effort
says,*

NARRATOR: Alright... but you must promise, and
I mean truly, genuinely promise me that you will
let me conduct the questioning.

WRATHER: Cross my heart and hope to die.

NARRATOR: No, I mean an oath on something
you hold sacred.

WRATHER: Fifty guineas...

NARRATOR: Fifty...?

WRATHER: I'll give you fifty guineas to hold, and
if I fail to meet your standards of decorum, then
let it be forfeit.

NARRATOR: Am I to understand from that there
is nothing you hold sacred?

WRATHER: I feel quite religious about fifty
guineas, I can assure you...

33 EXT. DRYING GREEN - DAY

The Narrator is with Mrs Brimley who is pegging out some bed linens on the line. He follows her through the flapping whites.

MRS BRIMLEY: What's between you two? He's been very short with me since you were last here...

NARRATOR: We quarrelled...

MRS BRIMLEY: Ah. Thought as much...so is this you wantin' to make up to him...?

NARRATOR: After a fashion, I suppose. Although I should scarcely know where to begin.

MRS BRIMLEY: Oh, begin at the end. Tell him whatever you said or did was your fault. You see that now, you're very sorry, won't ever happen again, and such like... That's what Albert did when he crossed me, and it always worked. Least ways about smoothing things over... So don't think you can apologize too much, Master Henslowe. You'd be surprised how much of it they'll put up with...

34   EXT. PARK - DAY

The Narrator is pushing his father along in the wheelchair. It's clear the Narrator has been going on for some time although Fisk Sr shows no signs of satiety.

NARRATOR: ...I can only imagine that I was not myself to have spoken to you in such a fashion and it grieves me to think I may have offended you by my lack of respect...

FISK: 'Sharper than a serpent's tooth,' you know...

NARRATOR: Yes, and I am stricken to think I have given you cause to think me ungrateful.

Fisk waves a hand imperiously.

FISK: Don't grovel laddie, you remind me of Wag when he'd been naughty. What a whining and squirming he went in for...

The Narrator casts about to place this reference, then, recalling,

NARRATOR: Ah, yes, Wag...

FISK: One of the seven great dogs. At any given time, you know, there are only seven great dogs alive. Wag was one of them...

~ 211 ~

Tailing off. They go along in silence a moment, then the Narrator asks,

NARRATOR: What happened to him...?

Fisk's face is suddenly still at the question, and he doesn't answer for a moment, then,

FISK: He went away one day and never came back...

NARRATOR: Had he ever done that before...?

FISK: Never... I blame the bad company he fell in with...this dog that used to come around. Ugly brute, a mongrel, big scrawny thing it was...Wag chased him off at first, but it came back and Wag took off with it...just before I had to return to school...I wanted to stay home till Wag came back. But they wouldn't allow it. I told them if I wasn't there, Wag might not know where to come to, but they wouldn't believe me...

He shakes his head, falls silent. The Narrator waits a moment, then,

NARRATOR: That must have been very difficult for you...

And Fisk looks round, eyes glittering,

FISK: It was unbearable...

And he looks away again and they trudge on a moment, then,

FISK: ...Yes, only seven at any one time. Why I never got another one. You're not going to be that lucky twice.

35 INT. APARTMENT - NIGHT

The Narrator is carefully decanting the Tokay. Wrather is looking around the apartment. He stops at the portrait over the fireplace.

WRATHER: Who is this likely looking lad?

NARRATOR: My brother Harrington. He was killed fighting the Boers...broke my mother's heart...

WRATHER: And Fisk Sr, how did he take it?

The Narrator looks up, stoney-faced.

NARRATOR: Whatever goes to the trouble of happening may be considered inevitable, was his comment I believe...

WRATHER: That's your stiff upper English for you..

He comes over, picks up the bottle which has an inch or so left in it. Starts to pour it in saying,

WRATHER: ...There's a few shillings left here...the cobwebs alone are worth a guinea...

But the Narrator stops him, saying,

NARRATOR: No, not the last inch...the Dean is very insistent on that.

WRATHER: Fussy old hound...what kind of dog did he say he was...?

And at that moment the doorbell goes and the Narrator shoots Wrather an alarmed look.

NARRATOR: He has not said and I must insist you do not ask him such a question...

WRATHER: I should have thought it the first thing that would occur to one to ask...like meeting an Army chap and not asking him his regiment.

NARRATOR: Your word, Wrather...

WRATHER: As you like, but I don't doubt I'll be able to tell as soon as he gets started...

As the Narrator goes into the vestibule to admit and greet Dean Spanley, Wrather, assessing himself in a mirror, goes on, saying,

WRATHER: ...I fancy I'd have been some kind of sight hunter, Afghan, Borzoi, something of that sort...

At the front door, the Narrator admits Dean Spanley.

NARRATOR: Ah, Dean, how good to see you...

He leads Spanley into the apartment to where Wrather, practising a wolfish grin, waits.

NARRATOR: Dean, this is my friend, Mr Wrather...

And seeing the look of concern in Spanley's eyes,

NARRATOR: ...Mr Wrather is the agent by which I have managed to procure the Tokay...

WRATHER: Good evening, Dean...

And the Dean, rather distantly, nods.

WRATHER: ...Yes, tonight's vintage is rather a special one... a Kleinfeld-Hasslerbeck...'82. One of the great years...

Somewhat mollified, the Dean approaches the sideboard where the decanted bottle stands by its freed contents.

DEAN SPANLEY: Indeed...I have never had the good fortune to sample this particular vintage.

WRATHER: Ah well, every dog has his day, as they say...

And the Narrator shoots him a glance, but Spanley seems oblivious, still fingering the bottle.

DEAN SPANLEY: My... what a privilege...

DISSOLVE TO:

36 INT. DINING ROOM - NIGHT

The meal has progressed to the Tokay stage and from the expression on Wrather's FACE, it has been singularly un-rewarding.

DEAN SPANLEY: Of course, the Empire must be maintained, but history shows only too clearly the dangers of over reach. Myself, I considered the Indian Mutiny so called a warning that perhaps our presence on the subcontinent was not the universal benevolence we supposed...

Wrather looks at the Narrator, who, aware that things are not yet ripe, says,

WRATHER: A glass of the Tokay, Dean...?

And with as close to a 'I'd thought you'd never ask' as he can allow himself, Spanley says,

DEAN SPANLEY: That would be most agreeable.

The Narrator rises, goes to the sideboard from where he hears Wrather say,

WRATHER: So Dean, do you think it's true that you can't teach an old dog new tricks...?

The Narrator turns hurriedly, decanter in hand, saying,

NARRATOR: I think what Mr Wrather means is...

And Wrather, amused at the intervention, goes on,

WRATHER: ...Will we ever give India back to the Indians...?

DEAN SPANLEY: Not in my lifetime, I would venture. We have come too much to depend on it...

And as the Narrator hastens to pour him a drink, looking daggers at Wrather, Spanley goes on,

DEAN SPANLEY: ...And I do not mean only economically, although we derive inordinate treasure from our exploitation of it...thank you...

As his glass is filled, his nose twitching over the rim,

DEAN SPANLEY: ...No, we also have become habituated to the role of Master and Dog, I mean, Servant...

And he breathes in the bouquet,

DEAN SPANLEY: ...Aah, how elegant...

The Narrator pours Wrather a smidgen, who indicates he wants more, and grudgingly, he complies as Spanley rhapsodizes,

DEAN SPANLEY: Oh my...oh, my, my...

And for a moment he is lost in rapture.

NARRATOR: Is it all you hoped, Dean?

DEAN SPANLEY: Beyond hope, beyond imagining. Actuality exceeds anticipation, leading to further anticipation... the perfect circle.

He looks at the Narrator, genuine gratitude shining in his eyes.

DEAN SPANLEY: I am in your debt, sir...

And then to Wrather,

DEAN SPANLEY: ...And yours, Mr Wrather.

NARRATOR: You were saying about the relationship between us and the Indians, one of Servant and Master...

DEAN SPANLEY: Not just servant and master, but Loving Servant. That is most important to the English race, that we are loved by those we rule...

WRATHER: With a dog-like devotion, would you say...?

The Narrator flinches at this latest example of Wrather's lack of tact. But Spanley takes the remark quite seriously.

DEAN SPANLEY: A term usually flavoured with pejorative connotations, but one, I might remind you, not inappropriate to the relationship between Man and God...

WRATHER: Who is, after all, but Dog spelled backwards...

And the Narrator kicks Wrather under the table, but again Spanley seems unperturbed.

DEAN SPANLEY: A curious inversion, indeed. A mirroring of some more profound truth, perhaps...in the English language, at least...

Wrather is now looking openly sceptical about the whole business and the Narrator, a trifle desperately, says,

NARRATOR: You were saying, about Master and...

And Spanley, suddenly there, in his other mind, replies with no hesitation.

DEAN SPANLEY: Yes, the Master. The thing is that whenever he returned from wherever he'd been, no matter how long one had waited, the actuality always exceeded the anticipation.

And the Narrator, risking all, adds,

NARRATOR: Causing you to run around in circles...

Spanley looks at him and after a moment, it seems as if the Narrator has overreached himself, then,

DEAN SPANLEY: Yes, most exhilarating...

And the Narrator looks triumphantly at Wrather who nods, beginning to be convinced, as Spanley goes on.

DEAN SPANLEY: ...Mind you, for all His great wisdom, there are certain things the Master did not understand...

Wrather gulps down his wine, and reaches for the decanter, as the Narrator says, conversationally, settling down to listen,

NARRATOR: Such as...?

DEAN SPANLEY: Oh...the moon...and ticks...

Wrather gulps another glass, getting a look from the Narrator, as Spanley nods to himself, sipping his wine, going on,

DEAN SPANLEY: ....The Master always wanted to remove mine. My own motto was live and let live...

WRATHER: Very Christian of you, I'm sure... but don't ticks hurt?

DEAN SPANLEY: No, no. Less than a flea bite. And once they are there, there they are, and if you wait till they drop off you can nip them up and have your blood back, strangely altered in flavour by having been bottled, as it were.

And he licks his lips in a little tug of recollection. The Narrator and Wrather have the same, queasy reaction to this but the Narrator shakes his head, a little warning negative. They wait until Spanley has finished this latest exploration of the Tokay, then the Narrator says,

NARRATOR: And the moon...?

DEAN SPANLEY: The moon...yes, the moon. The Master wasn't suspicious enough of the moon, in my opinion. Why it was always changing its shape and why it came sneaking up that way it did, over the hill, and why it had no smell...

And there is a CUT of the moon, almost full, coming over the horizon, then, BACK TO:

DEAN SPANLEY: I never trusted it. Never the same two nights in a row. And you could never hear it coming. If you can't hear a thing, you must be able to smell it...and I told it so...

And CUT TO a DOG barking at the moon, frantically, then BACK:

DEAN SPANLEY: ...in no uncertain terms. I told it to get off and it did. Every time...but always very slowly...

NARRATOR: Quite so...

Spanley looks at him as Wrather replenishes his glass, and then his own.

DEAN SPANLEY: Well, you can take your own line about that and others do. A friend of mine never worried about the moon, but he didn't have a house to guard and the moon had a way of looking at a house that implied it wasn't properly guarded...

And he nods to Wrather who stops pouring, goes on.

DEAN SPANLEY: ...The house was perfectly well guarded, and I said so, every time it came round, I said so in no uncertain terms...

Again, the DOG barking at the newly risen moon and a VOICE from the house calling it in, but the Dog pays no heed, continuing to shout out its warning, then BACK TO:

WRATHER: So you frightened it off...

Spanley shakes his head, nose over the glass.

DEAN SPANLEY: I don't think so. I don't think it was the least frightened. Which is surprising because it wasn't much bigger than my water dish and if I had been that size I would have been frightened of someone as big as me...

WRATHER: Oh, were you very big...?

DEAN SPANLEY: Oh yes...

And he takes a drink as the Narrator and Wrather exchange glances.

WRATHER: How big...?

DEAN SPANLEY: When I barked, I was enormous.

The Narrator, alarmed at Wrather taking the lead, says quickly,

NARRATOR: So why do you think it wasn't frightened?

DEAN SPANLEY: Frightened things smell frightened.

Spanley says in the tone of one explaining the obvious.

DEAN SPANLEY: ...I've smelled many frightened things. Cats, elderly ladies, children, rabbits, postmen, sheep. They all smell of being frightened. It's a wonderful smell...

WRATHER: You mean old ladies smell the same as rabbits when they're frightened?

The Narrator is concerned with the tone of Wrather's questioning, but Spanley seems not to notice.

DEAN SPANLEY: Their fear smells the same. Apart from that there's no confusing them.

And the Narrator comes in with his less aggressive tone,

NARRATOR: This business of smell is very interesting isn't it...?

DEAN SPANLEY: Interesting...?

And his expression is one of surprise at such a naive question. He browses a moment in the pastures of the Tokay, then,

DEAN SPANLEY: If I had to find fault with the Master, it would be on that issue...I have known occasions...

And WE SEE the DOG on a leash, its nose to the bole of a tree, being jerked away, and we HEAR:

DEAN SPANLEY (V.O.): ...I have been intent on a message left me by a friend when the Master would jerk me away in the middle of the most fascinating passage...

And WE ARE BACK WITH Wrather who says,

WRATHER: Rather like dragging a scholar away from a text in the British Museum...

Spanley's face registers a sudden confusion at this playback of his own remark, and the Narrator, seeing it, immediately comes in, again daggering a glance at Wrather.

NARRATOR: Perhaps that is an untoward analogy...

DEAN SPANLEY: No, no, most apposite...I have thought the same thing...I believe...

As doubt flickers in his eyes as to what he is saying.

DEAN SPANLEY: ...myself...

Tailing off uncertainly and, into this fissure Wrather again sticks his foot.

WRATHER: What sort of a dog were you, anyway?

And the state of mind, whatever it was, crumbles, leaving Spanley staring at him, puzzled, confused.

DEAN SPANLEY: I beg your pardon...?

Wrather sees he has broken the spell, tries to hearty it out.

WRATHER: In your day, I mean, before you took holy orders. Sowing wild pups, that sort of thing...?

And Spanley recovers his ecclesiastical gravitas, says, sniffily,

DEAN SPANLEY: I recall no such activities, I'm afraid...

CUT TO:

36A INT. APARTMENT - NIGHT

The Narrator has just seen Dean Spanley out. He comes back to where Wrather is still at the table, a glass of the Tokay before him, writing something. He looks up as the Narrator returns, sits down, a perplexed look on his face.

WRATHER: Quite a session that, damn good value...

The Narrator looks at him, shakes his head.

NARRATOR: It's all too outlandish. I mean, what is one to think? The man is clearly delusional...

He stares at his glass in which a certain quantity of the Tokay remains. He swirls it in the glass.

NARRATOR: ...As for this stuff, I hope I never acquire a taste for it. Hard to come by, and devilish expensive. Ten guineas to hear a Dean believe he was once a dog...I must be mad.

Something flutters over and lands in front of him. It's a cheque for fifty guineas. He looks at Wrather.

NARRATOR: What's this?

WRATHER: Good as gold...

The Narrator shakes his head, tosses the cheque back.

NARRATOR: I don't want your money. The whole thing has gone too far as it is...

WRATHER: Can't stop now, old man...

Getting up and coming round to stand behind him. The Narrator looks round.

NARRATOR: I can see no purpose in continuing. The man thinks he was a dog once and that's an end of it...

WRATHER: You're not one of those chaps who gives up before they can lose, are you?

The Narrator gets to his feet, offended by this remark, but Wrather goes on, genially.

WRATHER: How about if I procure some more of the elixir...?

NARRATOR: As I said, what more is to be gained by indulging the Dean in these ramblings...?

He tails off and Wrather says,

WRATHER: For free.

NARRATOR: For free...?

His voice incredulous.

WRATHER: And by the way, he was a Spaniel, the Dean. Always had an exaggerated opinion of themselves. 'When I barked, I was enormous.' That's Spaniels all over for you...

The Narrator, ignoring this remark, is caught by the offer.
NARRATOR: Where would you expect to find a free Imperial Tokay, Wrather...?

DISSOLVE TO:

40 EXT. THE NAWAB'S MANSION - DAY

The Narrator and Wrather coming up to the house in Wrather's car.

CUT TO:

40A INT. MANSION - DAY

They come through the foyer and we might notice that the menagerie has been added to by the presence of the warthog. They go to the ballroom.

41 INT. BALLROOM - DAY

The Nawab is at the nets. There are the same Figures in attendance. The Wicket Keeper, Umpire and two Bowlers. Wrather and The Narrator stand watching. The Nawab cuts fine to the next ball, plays forward and misses, is given out, leg before. He stifles a protest, walks from the wicket, comes out to the two men, saying to them once he is past the Umpire,

NAWAB: I thought that was going down the leg side...

NARRATOR: I rather agree.

WRATHER: Plumb in front...

The Nawab looks disgruntled.

NAWAB: I hate to lose a wicket just before tea. The new batsman has to play himself in twice...

WRATHER: Well, let's have tea now and you only have to play yourself in once.

The Nawab glances at the clock on the painted pavilion which is set at 10 minutes to 3 o'clock.

NAWAB: Yes, well, it's a bit of a cheat, but so was that decision...

He calls to the others in his charade.

NAWAB: Tea interval, chaps, twenty minutes.

And the Bowlers look at each other, raising their eyebrows.

1ST BOWLER: Doesn't want to play himself in twice...

Watching the Nawab walk away, bat under his arm.

2ND BOWLER: Mind you, I thought that one was going down leg side...

42 INT. CONSERVATORY - DAY

The Nawab, Wrather and the Narrator are sat down to tea.

NAWAB: Tokay, you say? An Imperial?

NARRATOR: Yes. We're finding it hard to come by.

NAWAB: I should jolly well think so. Rather extravagant to be so keen on it, I'd say...you must be quite the connoisseur.

WRATHER: It isn't for him...

Ignoring the Narrator's look, he goes on.

WRATHER: ...it's for Dean Spanley.

The Nawab looks surprised.

NAWAB: For Spanley? Old Wag Spanley likes Tokay...?

WRATHER: Very partial to a drop, the Dean is...

Looks at the Narrator for corroboration. The Narrator has a look of disbelief on his face.

THE FILM: SCREENPLAY

NARRATOR: Pardon me, Nawab, but did you call Dean Spanley 'Wag'...?

NAWAB: Walter Arthur Graham. Wag Spanley. Before my time, but my father knew him at Oxford. But tell me, why are you intent on plying him with Tokay, if you don't mind me asking?

The Narrator, still gathering his composure, says, vaguely,

NARRATOR: It has to do with one of the major tenets of your religion, sir...

NAWAB: Bat and pad together, when playing forward...?

WRATHER: Reincarnation, actually.

Seeing the Narrator pre-occupied with his thoughts.

NAWAB: Don't go in for it much, myself. I mean, I'm not going to do much better the next time round, am I...?

And he stands up. Starts toward the ballroom. The Narrator and Wrather follow, exchanging glances, as the Nawab goes on.

NAWAB: ...About as good as it gets, I'd say. Rich as a rajah, or nearly, play very well off my legs, shot almost everything that walks on all fours...

They go down the hallway,

NAWAB: ...And a few on two. No, this inning will do me nicely...

And they come to the entrance to the ballroom. The others are there waiting. The Nawab pauses,

NAWAB: ...Reincarnation is all right for the
masses, gives them something to look forward
to... About the Tokay, have a look in the cellar.
Galsworthy will show you around. There's all sorts
down there. Wouldn't be surprised if you found
the odd case of Tokay. Don't like the stuff myself.
Last time I drank it, I dreamt I was a monkey...

*And he walks to the wicket, to polite applause from the other
players.*

43 INT. WRATHER'S CAR - DAY

*Wrather driving. The Narrator stares out, his face a study in
the difficulties of thinking the unthinkable. There are several
bottles of the Tokay in a box on his knee.*

WRATHER: Thought he'd have a dozen or two lying around...

He looks over at the Narrator.

WRATHER: ...Ought to be enough there to get the old boy back to when he was a pup...

Notices his expression.

WRATHER: ...Cheer up, old man, might never happen. I've been thinking. Young lady I know, in the thespian way, thought we might take her a bottle of the Imperial...lovely girl, lot of fun when she's tight...

The Narrator seems not to have heard any of this for he cuts across Wrather's proposal with,

NARRATOR: My father had a dog when he was a boy... its name was Wag...

Wrather doesn't quite get it. The Narrator goes on.

NARRATOR: ...Walter Arthur Graham...Wag Spanley...don't you think that's significant...?

And Wrather takes this in, looks back at the road, then,

WRATHER: I think for that to be significant, you'd have to suppose two things, neither of them very probable to my mind... One, the Dean's mum and dad knew he had previously been your father's pooch, and, two, commemorated the event by incorporating his doggy name into his Christian one...

The Narrator nods, all this has already occurred to him. Wrather glances over, sees the set of his jaw as he stares out of the window.

WRATHER: No, it looks like a boat, but it won't float, as my Auntie Molly used to say...

And they go over a bump and the bottles of Tokay clink in the Narrator's lap. He stills them with his hand.

NARRATOR: Maybe there isn't enough Tokay under its keel...

And as Wrather goes on, a thought crosses the Narrator's mind that makes all the previous absurdities fade into insignificance.

CUT TO:

38 INT. FISK'S HOUSE - DAY

Fisk is in a chair being barbered by a talkative little BARBER. Fisk's face holds an expression of barely controlled irritation as the Barber makes barber talk.

BARBER: ...So I says to him, I says, well now that's as maybe, you may say so, but that's not the end of it...not by a long chalk...

He stops, considers his handiwork then in the gap created goes off at a tangent.

BARBER: ...Never understood that, 'a long chalk', what it means, like, would you know that, Mr Fisk...?

Starting to remove the apron from around Fisk's neck, brushing him down.

FISK: Is it not enough, Mr Collins, that I listen to your interminable, pointless ramblings without having to supply the meaning of esoteric idioms as well...?

And at that moment the Narrator ENTERS. The Barber, who seems not to have taken offence at this, turns to greet him.

BARBER: Ah, Young Mr Fisk...you wouldn't by chance know what 'a long chalk' means...?

NARRATOR: No, I'm afraid not, Mr Collins...

Looking intently at Fisk who is surveying his appearance in the mirror without great satisfaction.

BARBER: Well, never mind. I'll find out for next month, Mr Fisk. See if I don't...

And Fisk, still fussing with his hair, meets the Narrator's gaze, misinterpreting its scrutiny.

FISK: You look as if you had seen an apparition rather than an over-zealous hair cut...

NARRATOR: No, no, not at all...

The Barber has gathered up his gear.

BARBER: Right then. I'll be off...Mrs Brimley in the kitchen..?

Fisk glares at him.

FISK: Where else would Mrs Brimley be?

And undeterred, the Barber smiles, nods to the Narrator, leaves. Fisk shakes his head.

FISK: Always trying to ingratiate himself with Mrs Brimley...be proposing to her next.

NARRATOR: I think she is too comfortable with her memories of Albert's silences to be tempted by Mr Collins...

And as Fisk dons his jacket again, still primping at his hair,

NARRATOR: ...Father, there was something I was wondering...

Pausing, suddenly uncertain. Fisk looks round. The Narrator stands, hesitant. A moment passes, then Fisk, irritably,

FISK: Yes...? Or should I guess, perhaps?

NARRATOR: Your dog, the one you had when you were a boy...

FISK: Only dog I ever had. What about him?

NARRATOR: He was a spaniel...?

FISK: A Welsh Spaniel... none of your Cocker or Clumber or King Charles. One of the seven great dogs...

NARRATOR: Did he know when you were coming home...?

Fisk stares at him, surprised.

FISK: God bless my soul, what a question. Why do you ask...?

Embarrassed, the Narrator says,

NARRATOR: Oh, curiosity. I was just speaking to a chap whose dog knows when he is coming home...

Fisk nods, remembering, a little smile coming to his mouth.

FISK: Wag did, indeed. Would sit for hours, they told me, waiting. And long before I was in sight, would stand at the door, his stump thumping, and when I came in, he'd run round and round in circles... and then roll around on the floor as if he was drunk...he'd become quite dizzy, you see...

He cuts off his reminiscence, looks at the Narrator, suddenly suspicious.

FISK: ...What's got you interested in dogs of a sudden? Not thinking about getting one, I hope...

And before the Narrator can reassure him,

FISK: ...You're not the dog type...

And at this dismissal, the Narrator says defensively,

NARRATOR: Oh, and what type am I...?

Fisk looks at him a moment and the Narrator braces himself. Then,

FISK: More of a cat man, I'd say...

NARRATOR: In need of a snub to my vanity and ego...?

It's clear Fisk doesn't recall the origins of this remark. Shakes his head, back looking at his haircut.

FISK: I shouldn't go that far. Not by a long chalk...

NARRATOR: Whatever that means.

CUT TO:

44 INT. CLUB - DAY

The Narrator is with Spanley.

DEAN SPANLEY: A '79... Really my dear sir, you are a man of remarkable resource...

NARRATOR: Actually, it is not I who provided this trove... it is my father, whom I believe you've met. Indeed, it was he who introduced us...

DEAN SPANLEY: Oh, yes, I believe I do recall.

And it doesn't look like the happiest of memories.

NARRATOR: I was rather hoping he might join us at our next get together.

DEAN SPANLEY: I see...and your friend...Mr...

NARRATOR: Wrather...

DEAN SPANLEY: Wrather, yes...I have the strangest feeling, after our last encounter, that I know Mr Wrather, perhaps from a previous life, I was not always a Dean, you know...

And the Narrator stares, surprised at what seems to be a conscious acknowledgement of this whole business, until the Dean goes on.

DEAN SPANLEY: ...I was in social work at one time. A sorrowful business, at least in the regions where I toiled...

NARRATOR: And you think you may have met Wrather then...?

DEAN SPANLEY: It is possible. Or perhaps it's his being a colonial. One often feels one has met them before.

And he nods at this mysterious fact. The Narrator waits a moment, then,

NARRATOR: So may I hope for your company this Thursday evening? I feel only your palate can hope to do justice to a '79, Dean...

DEAN SPANLEY: ...A '79...well, well, what splendours that appellation conjures up... a bottle of the '79...

NARRATOR: Three bottles...

DEAN SPANLEY: Bless my soul, Mr Fisk, how does your father manage such a thing...?

CUT TO:

45 INT. STUDY - DAY

The Narrator with his father.

FISK: And why would I want to have dinner with a dean, let alone one who believes in reincarnation...

NARRATOR: You are always complaining that I neglect you for my evenings with Spanley. I thought you might want to join us...Wrather will be with us... You remember him, the conveyancer, from the lecture...?

Fisk shakes his head.

FISK: Can't say as I do...

Then, abruptly,

FISK: It must be here, this gathering. Certainly not at that rickety place of yours...

NARRATOR: Can Mrs Brimley cook for four...?

FISK: She can make more of her hot pot.

NARRATOR: We are having a Shevenitz-Donetschau '79...I do not think the hot pot, sustaining though it undoubtedly is, is quite the precursor to a '79 Tokay...

FISK: Damn fuss over fermented grapes. What is this all to do with... the Dean, the Tokay, this dinner...?

NARRATOR: If I were to tell you, Father, you would not believe me.

FISK: In that case, don't tell me. I don't believe in enough things already...

46 INT. KITCHEN - DAY

The Narrator has just informed her of the event to come, and Mrs Brimley, looking not un-pleased, is saying,

MRS BRIMLEY: Well, it won't be the hot pot, is all I can say. I'm not serving hot pot to a Dean, what would he think of your father...

NARRATOR: Why not prepare your Navarin? The Dean appreciates a lamb stew. I've always had a great success with your recipe...

MRS BRIMLEY: Did you do it with shallots and tarragon...?

NARRATOR: Just as you showed me.

MRS BRIMLEY: I *could* do the Navarin. With that sorrel and cucumber soup to start. Or maybe the leek'n potato, what your father calls the 'vicious-swiss' soup...

NARRATOR: Either, I think, would be most welcome...

Mrs Brimley has already brought out her recipe book. The Narrator watches her a moment, then,

NARRATOR: Mrs Brimley...

She is looking through pages, almost purring at the prospects opening up. He waits a moment, then,

NARRATOR: ...Mrs Brimley, do you remember my father's dog, Wag? A spaniel it was...

MRS BRIMLEY: ...And for dessert, profiteroles. My choux pastry is too good to be eaten, even if I says so myself... Hmm...?

Looking up at him, just hearing the question.

MRS BRIMLEY: ...Wag? No, not really. I remember it run off, though. What a to-do that was. Like a death in the family. Upset him ever so. Why didn't he get another, I asked him once. Know what he said...?

NARRATOR: That Wag was one of the seven great dogs...?

MRS BRIMLEY: I see he's talked to you about it...

And she goes back to her recipes, fussing already.

MRS BRIMLEY: Maybe profiteroles would be too heavy after the lamb. Something lighter, more tart, raspberry and gooseberry fool...

And the Narrator leaves her, saying only,

NARRATOR: Whatever you decide, Mrs Brimley, I'm sure will be splendid...

47 INT. BILLIARD ROOM - DAY

The Narrator and Wrather. This time it's the Narrator who is playing solitaire. Wrather stands deep in thought as the Narrator stalks around potting ball after ball. We should note that instead of his usual neckwear, the Narrator sports a more casual cravat, a sartorial touch that continues for the duration.

WRATHER: You sure this is a good idea, young Henslowe? Might be best to let sleeping dogs lie, if you know what I mean...

The Narrator looks at him, nods.

NARRATOR: Yes, I know what you mean...

WRATHER: Might take it amiss, is all I'm saying. What if he were to recognize your father, start licking his hands or some such... Be damned embarrassing...

The Narrator pauses to consider this, then, in the grip of his dream,

NARRATOR: Pygmy judge, old man, Pygmy judge...

And crashes a final ball home.

DISSOLVE TO:

WRATHER
FISK-JNR-
FISK-SNR-
(Twisted in his chair away from dean for first part of conversation)
DEAN
(sitting on a smaller chair)

48 INT. DINING ROOM - EVENING

Fisk is in full flow as the Narrator pours the evening's first glass of Tokay for the table.

FISK: ...So there we were, on our holidays in this cottage on the shore of Windermere. Wonderful spot to get some reading done, and I was availing myself of the tranquillity to do just that. This fellow here, Young Fisk, and his brother, were out on the lake in a rowboat. Storm came up, as they do, you know. One minute it's all I wandered lonely as a cloud, the next it's blowing hell's bells and howling like a banshee. So, Mrs Fisk, she comes in, wringing her hands. 'The boys,' she cries at me, 'they're out on the lake.' You have no idea how taxing it is to be dragged out of a book you're thoroughly immersed in. Rather like dragging a dog away from a lamp post...

Which, in various ways, gets everybody's attention, even Spanley raising his nose from his glass as Fisk goes on.

FISK: ...'You must do something, Horatio,' she says. 'Our sons are in great danger. Do something, do something,' she implored me. So, I got up, laying aside Balzac with the greatest reluctance, and I went to the window, opened the shutters. Well, it was a regular Gustav Doré engraving out there, I can tell you. White caps as far as the eye could see, lightning flashes, cracking thunder. I stared out into the maelstrom and I raised my hands and called out in my most stentorian tone, 'Give up your dead, give up your dead.'

And there is a little silence at this, into which the Narrator, says,

NARRATOR: Which was a great comfort to my mother, as you can imagine...

FISK: When one is helpless, I see no point in pretending otherwise...

WRATHER: Still, all's well that turns out all right... you'n your brother made it back to shore.

The Narrator refills the Dean's glass, which is the only one empty, saying,

NARRATOR: We were blown across to the other side, bailing all the way, didn't get back till morning.

DEAN SPANLEY: How terrible that must have been for your mother...

And he glances quickly at Fisk,

DEAN SPANLEY: ...and you too, sir...

FISK: When something goes to the trouble of happening, it's best to consider it inevitable, in my opinion. Learned that lesson the hard way, I did.

NARRATOR: Well, let us drink to the inevitable, before it happens.

And with varying shades of dubiety, the others drink. Wrather nods approvingly.

WRATHER: Not a bad drop...I'm beginning to get the hang of this stuff.

FISK: Too much like toilet water for my taste...

Spanley is as ever lost in the enchanted caverns of his nose and the expression on his face is blissful.

DEAN SPANLEY: Oh my, oh my...

He looks around the table, a little dazed with delight, as Fisk rings the dinner bell, summoning Mrs Brimley.

DEAN SPANLEY: My dear sir...

As Mrs Brimley COMES IN, stands quietly, as Spanley goes on.

DEAN SPANLEY: ...You are to be congratulated... as is your chef. A meal fit for a Tokay...

Fisk looks at Mrs Brimley.

FISK: You can clear away now, Mrs Brimley...

Then, to Spanley,

FISK: ...She does a very good hot pot, I should tell you...

Mrs Brimley stares daggers at him as he goes on, indicating the Tokay,

FISK: ...We'll take this in the drawing room...

DEAN SPANLEY: If you wouldn't mind, sir, I should prefer to remain here to enjoy my Tokay...

FISK: Oh, and why's that, then?

DEAN SPANLEY: I cannot really say...

And he puts his nose back in his glass and Fisk Sr looks askance at the Narrator as Mrs Brimley stands, waiting. Wrather sensing an impending rupture in the fabric, says,

WRATHER: Sometimes you get comfortable where you are. Don't like to disturb yourself...

FISK: Poppycock. Port should be taken in the study, let the ladies get on with whatever it is they get on with...

And the Narrator tries to get a conciliatory remark in before it all goes sideways.

NARRATOR: In this case, Father, there are no ladies to consider...

Then remembering Mrs Brimley's presences, adds,

NARRATOR: ...Aside from Mrs Brimley, of course.

MRS BRIMLEY: I'm no lady. I just want to know...

Just then Dean Spanley speaks from his glass, a reverential air of recall in his voice.

DEAN SPANLEY: It is rather like being bathed when one has just gotten comfortable in one's smell.

Both Wrather and the Narrator know the tone, but Fisk Sr stares at him, bristling with incomprehension. Then, to the Narrator,

FISK: What's the fellow on about...?

But the Dean, seemingly not having heard Fisk, comes in with a tone of affectionate recollection in his voice.

DEAN SPANLEY: There was a patch of ground out behind the shed where the earth was always moist, and I loved to roll there to get that particular aura about me. It brought out the natural secretions so you could feel a glow all around oneself, like a halo...

And Fisk stares at him as if he'd gone mad, and the look on Mrs Brimley's face suggests the same thought. The Narrator says to her, in a whisper

NARRATOR: You can leave the clean up for now, Mrs Brimley...

*And she leaves, with a look of consternation for the Dean, who,
now well down the tunnel, is going on.*

DEAN SPANLEY: ...It would be then, just when one
felt so complete, that the Master would call me...

FISK: Who, in God's name, called you what...?

*In a tone meant to put an end to this nonsense. Spanley looks
at him, calm in his remembering.*

DEAN SPANLEY: The Master. He called me
Wag. For reasons I never understood. Wag.
You couldn't imagine that a single meaningless
syllable could convey so much. But that was the
greatness of the Master, that he could make that
one sound convey so many meanings... There was
a 'Wag' which meant 'a walk,' and a 'Wag' that
meant 'go away from the table,' and a 'Wag' that
meant, 'you are to be bathed,' and of all the
'Wags' that 'Wag' was the most terrible...

*Fisk is staring open-mouthed now, and the Narrator jumps in
to cover this astonishment and what it might lead to.*

NARRATOR: Why was that?

DEAN SPANLEY: Because for all his great wisdom,
he never seemed to understand how
embarrassing it is to meet another dog when one
wasn't wearing one's own smell...

WRATHER: Like not knowing who you were...

DEAN SPANLEY: Indeed. But more importantly,
they did not know who you were, and you had to
go through all that business of sniffing and
circling and growling...

*And we SEE two Dogs, A SPANIEL and a big-boned
MONGREL, doing just that, and this HOLDS AS WE
HEAR:*

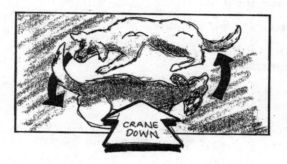

DEAN SPANLEY (V.O.): ...I was always being
embarrassed in that way with a particular friend
of mine...

WRATHER (V.O.): So what did you do...did you
have to fight him?

DEAN SPANLEY (V.O.): Oh, we fought a few times,
just to get acquainted...that I enjoyed...

*The two dogs go at each other in a tangle, snapping and
snarling.*

DEAN SPANLEY (V.O.): ...My favourite grip was the
ear. You hear that going for the throat is the best
approach, but in my experience it's almost
impossible to get a throat grip, so I would always
go for the ears...

*And we are BACK in the dining room where Fisk is staring,
still astonished, and now partially drawn into the narrative.*

FISK: But isn't the ear grip very painful?

DEAN SPANLEY: Not if you are the one who is doing the gripping.

FISK: Oh, yes, of course...

DEAN SPANLEY: Otherwise, it can be quite distressing...

WE CUT TO the two dogs, one of whom is yelping pathetically and we HEAR:

DEAN SPANLEY (V.O.): ...But it provides an opportunity for making an excellent complaint...

And the yelping grows more and more pathetic as Dean Spanley's VOICE continues:

DEAN SPANLEY (V.O.): ...My friend had a very good complaint which I memorized and used myself when I had to have a beating from the Master...

And we COME BACK TO the NARRATOR staring at Fisk, then,

NARRATOR: He beat you...?

FISK: Only when...

Then he stops himself as Spanley goes on,

DEAN SPANLEY: ...On certain occasions it was called for, and I would use this splendid complaint I learned from my friend...

WRATHER: What was his name, this friend of yours...?

DEAN SPANLEY: His name? I never knew what his Master called him. In truth, I was not entirely sure he had a master, but his complaint was most satisfying...

And we CUT TO the dogs, one of whom is still giving out a series of plaintive yelps which Spanley translates as:

DEAN SPANLEY (V.O.): Oh, rescue me, I am a poor unfortunate creature, misunderstood and cruelly used, far from home and without a friend...

And BACK TO the dining table as he continues.

DEAN SPANLEY: Help me, help me, for I have fallen into terrible straits and am soon to be murdered...

He smiles, all the while nose to the glass.

DEAN SPANLEY: ...Which, of course, was not the case.

And Fisk, says, almost embarrassedly, but unable to constrain himself,

FISK: This dog, the one you say had no master, what sort of dog was he...?

Spanley looks at him, eyes bright with recall and affection.

DEAN SPANLEY: Why, the best of fellows, fearless and bold, adventurous and carefree...

And drawn further in by this pronouncement,

FISK: But you said he was whining and snivelling about being murdered...

DEAN SPANLEY: Oh, that was just his complaint.

As if that explained everything, and suddenly Fisk pours himself a large glass of the Tokay which causes the Narrator to get up and bring the second decanter to the table.

WRATHER: How did you meet him, this friend of yours...?

DEAN SPANLEY: He used to leave messages on the cart which brought the milk. And I would reply...

CUT TO the Spaniel lifting its leg on the wheel of a horse-drawn cart, then CUT BACK.

DEAN SPANLEY: And then one day he came to our door.

And WE SEE THE ARRIVAL of the newcomer, rangy and ragged, and the Spaniel, from within the precincts of his house, barking wildly. We HEAR:

DEAN SPANLEY (V.O.): I told him to go away, or else I would chase him, and I barked my most enormous bark and made myself very large, but he wasn't afraid and said so...

The two dogs bark at each other vehemently for a time and then WE CUT BACK TO FIND FISK with an expression of alarm on his face, and something more, dissolving disbelief, in his eyes.

The Narrator is pouring more Tokay.

WRATHER: And what happened...?

DEAN SPANLEY: I got out...our house was very secure, but a dog who wants to get out can always do so...

And WE ARE WITH the Spaniel, wriggling through a gap in the fence to join the newcomer, and THEN BACK TO THE TABLE:

DEAN SPANLEY: And we met. I had just been bathed, so I was most embarrassed, but after we had a good fight, I felt much better...but unfortunately I was called in by the Master...

WE HOLD ON FISK'S FACE, while we hear a BOY'S VOICE calling,

VOICE (V.O.): Wag, come here, come here at once!

And CUT TO the Spaniel running back, reluctant, yet eager to crouch by the legs of a BOY whose features we don't see, and who continues to shout at the other dog which finally lopes away from the house.

WRATHER (V.O.): Was that the last you saw of him?

CUT TO Spanley.

DEAN SPANLEY: Oh no, for he came the next day, and the days after.

Wrather looks hesitant for a moment, then says,

WRATHER: I say, you weren't, how shall I put it, a female by any chance...?

FISK: Of course he wasn't.

But Spanley seems not to hear, although the Narrator does.

DEAN SPANLEY: Not at all. We were just good friends. He had lived a very interesting life and knew many more things than I did, which he told me about in considerable detail...

NARRATOR: Told you about...how?

Spanley looks at him, eyebrows raised in mild surprise.

DEAN SPANLEY: Why, in the messages he sent me.

And once more we SEE the Spaniel sniffing the cart wheel and then adding his own story, as:

DEAN SPANLEY (V.O.): ...And I would send him word of my doings which, I confess, were not comparable to his, for I only ever walked with the Master of an evening...

And we SEE THEM, figures in a landscape, the Spaniel close to heel.

DEAN SPANLEY (V.O.): ...And while they were enjoyable outings, they were but a mooncast shadow to his adventures...

And WE ARE BACK with them around the table, Spanley deep in his recall; Wrather glued to his every word; Fisk looking more uneasy by the minute, and the Narrator almost detached, watching, as it were, from a distance, his father as much as Spanley.

WRATHER: Did you ever go on an adventure with him?

DEAN SPANLEY: Indeed, the greatest of my life...

He nods, reaching absently for the decanter which Wrather hastily hands to him.

DEAN SPANLEY: Oh yes, a day to remember, it was. I remember the Master had to go away and I couldn't go with him...

And we SEE the Spaniel locked in a room, whining and scratching at the door, then stopping at the approach of steps. The door is opened and a Servant comes in, and the Spaniel slips out.

DEAN SPANLEY (V.O.): ...But I was going to follow him, only my friend came...

And we SEE the other dog come up to the gate and Wag runs down to meet him. They sniff each other, tails agog.

DEAN SPANLEY (V.O.): ...And he proposed we have an adventure and since the Master was going away, I agreed and off we went...

And we see them go trotting off together, and CUT BACK TO the table where all, in their various ways, are intent on Spanley.

He is wreathed in recall, a beatific expression on his face, which, unless we are much mistaken, has begun to take on a subtly doggish look.

DEAN SPANLEY: What a day that was to be a dog and to be with a dog who knew how to be one for I confess that happy though I was to belong to the Master, I had, until that day, barely glimpsed the glories of dog-dom...

And WE CUT TO the two dogs in full gallop along a hedgerow. We HEAR:

DEAN SPANLEY (V.O.): ...He introduced me to the joys of chasing animals, a matter in which I was largely unversed, having previously only had the opportunity to chase an occasional cat. Cats, you know, are of little use for chasing as, not knowing the rules, they invariably run up trees, a habit I find contemptible...

CUT TO the two dogs chasing a horse across a field.

DEAN SPANLEY (V.O.): ...Horses on the other hand, understand the rules perfectly, and enter into the business in good spirit. The important thing to remember in chasing horses is that it is the back of them you must be careful, whereas with cows...

AND WE CUT TO see the dogs trying to get a bunch of cows to start running without much success, the cows moving only to keep their tormentors in sight.

DEAN SPANLEY (V.O.): ...It is the front of them that is to be allowed for. Cows do not enjoy being chased as much as horses, but at least they do not climb trees. So we told them how cow-ish and stupid they were not to join in and left them...

And we see the dogs trot on, tongues lolling, happy in their depredations.

DEAN SPANLEY (V.O.): ...in search of better sport.

CUT TO a small flock of sheep, grazing on a hillside, as we HEAR:

DEAN SPANLEY (V.O.): ...I do not think that it can be disputed that of all the creatures a dog can chase, none exceeds sheep for sheer pleasure. For a start, they can do you no harm, either the front or back of them, and for another they grow infinitely more frightened than either horses or cows. Their fear drifts in clouds behind them and you breathe it in as you run so that you grow quite intoxicated by it. It is as if one was not so much running as flying on it. Or perhaps swimming would be a more exact description...

And we see, FROM A DISTANCE, the dogs chasing the sheep, twisting and turning after them.

DEAN SPANLEY (V.O.): And were it not that their Master appeared, we might have chased them all day...

And the figure of the SHEPHERD appears and chases the dogs, yelling and waving his arms.

DEAN SPANLEY (V.O.): ...My friend did not care, but I felt perhaps we might be seized and prevented from further adventures, so I persuaded him to leave...

We see the Spaniel heading off, but the other dog stands his ground, barking defiantly at the Shepherd, whose wrath now includes stone throwing, one such missile catching the dog and making it yelp before sloping off to join the Spaniel.

WE CUT BACK TO THE TABLE, where all are, despite variations of expressions, equally enthralled by this narrative.

The Narrator fills Spanley's glass as he continues, seemingly beyond interruption now.

DEAN SPANLEY: And so we continued. We found a pig in a pen and told it what an ugly, stupid, odorous creature it was. Many times we told it to its face...

AND WE CUT TO SEE the dogs barking into a sty, working up a lather at the pig's frantic attempts to get at them. We HEAR:

DEAN SPANLEY (V.O.): ...And when we had told it enough, and made it very angry, we left it to wonder why it wasn't a dog which I'm sure must be a source of great annoyance to it, and we went into the woods. There, we had the good fortune to come upon a rabbit...

And WE SEE the creature, startled and dashing into a thicket.

DEAN SPANLEY (V.O.): ...It is not commonly known that rabbit scent, particularly when it is frightened, and this rabbit was very frightened indeed...

And a SHOT OF THE RABBIT, deep in the undergrowth.

DEAN SPANLEY (V.O.): ...It does not lie along the ground, but rises in heaps so that you must jump to inhale it...

And the two dogs run around the thicket the rabbit is hiding in, leaping and barking.

DEAN SPANLEY (V.O.): When we'd had our fill of its fear, which is a wonderful flavour, sweeter than sheep fear, and stronger than cats', we turned to catching it, and in this endeavour my friend showed what a remarkable fellow he was, for he drove through the thicket giving no heed to its many inconveniences and sent the rabbit scuttling to where I was stationed...

And we see the rabbit come bursting out, only to be snapped up by the Spaniel, caught and shaken dead. Then the other dog comes out and seizes its hindquarters and they tug on it, savagely, growling and snarling until the creature tears in half, and they retire with a piece each.

DURING THIS NARRATIVE, at some point WE CUT to find Mrs Brimley standing outside the dining room door, listening, look of bewilderment on her face, and at the appropriate moment she throws up her hands and walks off, shaking her head as...

Then CUT BACK TO Dean Spanley, going on.

DEAN SPANLEY (V.O.): ...I cannot describe how much more satisfying a recently alive rabbit tastes than the way I had previously encountered it. I'm afraid the Masters fail entirely to appreciate fur, bones and guts for the delicacies they are...

The dogs devour the whole rabbit, leaving no trace of its existence, save in their contented expressions.

DEAN SPANLEY (V.O.): It was then time to quench our thirst...

And we see them find a puddle among the trees, of brackish, muddy water which they lap up.

DEAN SPANLEY (V.O.): ...And we were fortunate, as in everything that befell us that glorious day, to find water gathered in a hollow and after we drank our fill, we rolled in it to give ourselves a glow, and then we went into the woods to rest in the shade...

And we see them find a spot under a tree and settle down, a few feet apart to groom and relish themselves, and WE COME BACK TO the table where the enchanted listeners wait to see just how much further the Dean will take them.

He seems to be resting, echoing his recollection and there is a silence into which Fisk says, trying to recover his equilibrium,

FISK: Perhaps we should move into the...

Only for two sets of glares, from the Narrator and Wrather, to silence him. He is taken aback, then, asserting himself, rising,

FISK: Well, suit yourselves, but I think...

NARRATOR: Sit where you are, Father...

His voice almost stern, and Fisk sits back down, and Wrather, hard on the heels of this, asks Spanley,

WRATHER: And what happened then...?

DEAN SPANLEY: Oh, we went to sleep, that most sublime of states, when a dream dreams you instead of the other way round...

And WE CUT TO A CLOSE of the Spaniel, asleep, whimpering in his excitement, and then BACK TO SPANLEY AT THE TABLE.

DEAN SPANLEY: ...And when we awoke, the moon was rising...

And WE CUT TO A huge moon coming over the horizon and spilling through the trees and we HEAR:

DEAN SPANLEY (V.O.): ...It was just on the other side of the wood, and so we set about surprising it...

The two dogs go through the trees, stalking towards the moon which has yet to clear the earth's rim.

DEAN SPANLEY (V.O.): We came very close to catching it for it was slow to get up, but when we were almost upon it, my friend could contain himself no longer and let out his cry...

And a HOWL goes up and the two dogs streak through the trees as the moon hoists itself into the sky until they come out of the woods on a bare hillside, and see the moon floating free across the valley. We HEAR:

DEAN SPANLEY (V.O.): ...And had we been but a moment sooner, we surely would have seized it, head and hind, and torn it apart as we had the rabbit. How it would have tasted, I cannot say, though it could scarcely have exceeded our last meal for succulence...

And we see the two dogs howling at the moon, as:

DEAN SPANLEY (V.O.): So we told it what a great cowardly, un-smelling thing it was and if we ever caught up with it, it would regret ever venturing our way, and when we saw it had no intention of coming back, we turned and went home...

FISK (V.O.): So you knew how to get home...?

And we CUT BACK TO FISK, waiting for an answer, entirely earnest, finally absorbed by the veracity of the Dean's story. The Narrator watches, concerned lest it interfere with the Dean's mood, but he seems unperturbed.

DEAN SPANLEY: Oh, yes, you just turn towards home and go there.

FISK: But you had been out all day, running free...how far from home were you?

DEAN SPANLEY: Oh, we had come many overs, it is true. I cannot say how many...

FISK: 'Overs'...?

DEAN SPANLEY: Yes, overs. Many overs...over fields, and hills, over streams and woods. Many overs...

FISK: And you just turned towards home...?

Spanley looks a little puzzled at this scepticism.

DEAN SPANLEY: How else would one do it...?

FISK: Hmmph... then why...

And tailing off as Spanley goes on.

DEAN SPANLEY: And I knew I should be beaten, and I remembered my friend's complaint that I

would use and how delicious it would feel after
the beating was over and the insults had stopped.
It was always worth it for that golden time after
you have been punished for your wrong-doing
and can feel the glow of well being that comes
with having paid the price...

*And WE SEE the two dogs now, dark shapes on a moonlit
field, go loping back and then WE ARE BACK WITH FISK,
asking, his voice a little tremulous,*

FISK: And were you... punished?

DEAN SPANLEY: No, not on that occasion.

FISK: Why was that... do you know?

DEAN SPANLEY: Because a very remarkable thing
occurred on the way back which I cannot
properly explain...

*And WE SEE THE dogs come down over the hill where they
chased the sheep, although they are no longer there.*

DEAN SPANLEY (V.O.): ...One moment we were
running, side by side, making our way home, and
the next we were not...

And we SEE IT THROUGH the dogs' eyes until abruptly, and with a single smash of SOUND, the screen goes BLACK, and we're BACK in the dining room and Wrather says,

WRATHER: Bugger shot him...

Said almost into his glass and to prove it we have the briefest of CUTS TO the Shepherd we saw earlier firing a shotgun and a GLIMPSE of the Spaniel hurled bloodily sideways, then BACK TO Spanley who is staring at Wrather, not quite comprehending.

DEAN SPANLEY: I do not know what happened. Perhaps it was a dream and I wakened from it...

FISK: Was there... any pain...?

Spanley tries to remember, shakes his head,

DEAN SPANLEY: Pain? No, I cannot say there was. I only remember how clear the night was with the moon-cast shadows and the earth springing up under me, and home in my heart and the Master waiting...

And he has come to the end of his recall again, shaking his head, puzzled.

DEAN SPANLEY: ...And then all at once it was gone... but no, no pain...

Fisk Sr has been watching him the while, his eyes bright and believing. He reaches out and pats the Dean's hand in a curious little intimacy, standing up as he does so.

FISK: I am most glad to hear it...if you will excuse me...

And starts to rise. Spanley, affected by the emotion he senses in his host which brings him back to a state of bewilderment, asks,

DEAN SPANLEY: Did I say something to upset you, sir...

Fisk looks down at him, deep, inexpressible affection in his eyes.

FISK: No, no, not at all...I am put in memory of my son... Harrington... that is all...

And he leaves them, suddenly intent on being alone. There is a little silence, into which the Narrator says,

NARRATOR: Harrington was killed in the Boer War. He was returning from a patrol...

He stops, himself affected, then,

NARRATOR: ...That is all we know. His body was never recovered...

And the three of them sit there in a silent moment of memorial.

49 INT. HALLWAY - NIGHT

Fisk stands in the hallway, his shoulders shaking, but fighting back his grief.

The Parlour door opens and Mrs Brimley comes out, sees Fisk.

MRS BRIMLEY: Are you all right, Mr Fisk...?

He looks at her, unable to speak. She comes out, solicitous.

FISK: He...was...he was...shot...

MRS BRIMLEY: Yes, a bad business it was that war. They're all bad business you ask me. Hope we don't have no more of them...

And Fisk is sobbing now and Mrs Brimley takes his arm.

MRS BRIMLEY: ...There, there, better late than never, Mr Fisk...come into the kitchen, and sit in Albert's chair and I'll make you a cup of tea...

As Fisk lets himself be led inside.

49A INT. KITCHEN - NIGHT

Mrs Brimley and Fisk come in. He seems lost, looks around as if he didn't know where he was. Mrs Brimley goes to the stove.

MRS BRIMLEY: Sit down, Mr Fisk, I'll put the kettle on...

He looks at the mantelpiece sees the photograph of his two long ago sons, goes over as Mrs Brimley puts the kettle on.

MRS BRIMLEY: ...Quite the story teller, that Dean of yours...

She glances over to where Fisk has picked up the photograph and stands staring at it.

MRS BRIMLEY: Lovely lads they were...

Fisk nods, touches the photograph with a tentative finger as behind him, over the clatter of cups, Mrs Brimley says,

MRS BRIMLEY: ...And one of them still is.

Fisk nods, puts the photograph back, looks round, eyes soft, pained.

FISK: Yes, yes, indeed...

MRS BRIMLEY: Sit down, Mr Fisk...

He moves towards a chair, sits down, almost wearily. After a moment, he says,

FISK: Do you remember Wag, Mrs Brimley...my dog...?

MRS BRIMLEY: No, what I remember is running after you when you went back to school and you looked round at me...I've never forgot your face...

And WE ARE ON Fisk as he remembers.

MRS BRIMLEY: ...I wondered what you had done to deserve such punishment, sent away like that...

Fisk nods, smiles.

FISK: Yes, Mrs Brimley. I too...

~ 269 ~

DISSOLVE TO:

50 INT. FOYER - NIGHT

Spanley and Wrather have their coats on. The Narrator comes through from the study. Wrather has a bottle of the Tokay in his hand.

NARRATOR: I think my father must have gone to bed...

DEAN SPANLEY: I hope whatever I said did not upset him...

And at that moment the parlour door opens and Fisk comes out, composed if a trifle wan.

FISK: Excuse me, I was talking to Mrs Brimley...about the old days. Thank you, Dean, for coming. It was a memorable evening...

DEAN SPANLEY: My pleasure, sir, though I rather feel the Tokay rendered me somewhat unsociable. It gives me a tendency to withdraw into myself...

FISK: Not at all...you were all that could be hoped for in a guest. You know your way home from here...?

Spanley looks askance at this, and Fisk takes his hand,

FISK: ...Just turn towards it, is the best way, I'm told...

But this doesn't register with Spanley.

WRATHER: I'm going in the Dean's direction. I'll see he gets there this time...

And the Narrator, eager to close this chapter, shoots Wrather a look, and says,

NARRATOR: Good night, Dean...

DEAN SPANLEY: Yes, good night...

And he and Wrather go, leaving father and son in the doorway, looking after their guests as they go down to the steps.

51 EXT. FISK HOUSE - NIGHT

As they walk away, Wrather hands the bottle to Dean Spanley.

WRATHER: Thought you might like one of these... as a little memento.

Spanley is overwhelmed.

DEAN SPANLEY: My dear sir. How very extravagant of you... does Mr Fisk...

WRATHER: Too shy to give it to you himself.

DEAN SPANLEY: Well, well, such generosity...

They walk a moment, then Spanley says,

DEAN SPANLEY: You know, Mr Wrather, I have the most persistent notion that we have met before...

WRATHER: One often feels that way with Colonials...

DEAN SPANLEY: So I have heard it said. Nevertheless...

Then he falls to gazing at the bottle of Tokay,

DEAN SPANLEY: My, my...

WRATHER: Ever thought of owning a parrot, Dean?

DEAN SPANLEY: A parrot, no. What makes you ask, Mr Wrather...?

CUT TO:

52 INT. FISK HOUSE - FOYER

Fisk and the Narrator, watching as the two men disappear into the dark, still absorbing the enormity of the evening. Then, Fisk, closing the door on their fading voices, says,

FISK: He can put away the Tokay, I'll say that for the Dean...

NARRATOR: Yes, I thought we might have to open the third bottle for a moment...

FISK: Oh, I think two was ample...he goes on a bit when he's in his cups, though...

The Narrator gets his coat and to his surprise, finds his father helping him on with it.

NARRATOR: Thank you, Father...

His back to Fisk, who smoothes out the shoulders.

FISK: One moment you're running along, the next you're no more...

The Narrator turns to look at him.

NARRATOR: At least he felt no pain...

FISK: Yes, we must hope so...

And he looks at his son, says in lieu of outright affection,

FISK: I like the cravat... rather rakish.

NARRATOR: Wrather's influence, I think...

FISK: Not as rakish as that. Bit of a remittance man, your friend Wrather...

NARRATOR: Yes, rather...

And they smile at each other.

NARRATOR: Until next Thursday then...

And abruptly he embraces Fisk, who holds him tight a moment, then steps back.

FISK: Or any day that suits. Mustn't get too set in our ways...good night, Henslowe...

NARRATOR: Good night, Father...

And he goes. Fisk closes the door, stands a moment, then he goes down the corridor. Stops at Mrs Brimley's door, listens.

He can hear her talking in a low, conversational tone.

MRS BRIMLEY (V.O.): God knows what they were on about, something about rabbits tasting better with the fur on them... you'll not find me cooking them, that's all I know...

And Fisk smiles, goes on down the corridor as she continues.

MRS BRIMLEY: ...Then he comes in here must be the first time in God knows how long and he stands looking at that photograph sobbin' his heart out...funny how it takes some people, now me, I bawled for a week after you was gone and that was it over with...

DISSOLVE TO:

53 EXT. HOUSE - MORNING

The Narrator comes up to the door, knocks, stands looking around until Mrs Brimley opens the door.

NARRATOR: Good morning, Mrs Brimley...

MRS BRIMLEY: It's not Thursday, you know.

NARRATOR: No, I know...

He steps in.

NARRATOR: ...How is my father...?

MRS BRIMLEY: Well, I don't rightly know...

And at that moment the SOUND of barking, high excited barking comes through to them. The Narrator stares at her. She nods.

MRS BRIMLEY: Wasn't my idea, mind you. Day after that dinner party, he has me go and see that friend of yours, the one was here...

NARRATOR: Mr Wrather...?

MRS BRIMLEY: Had me go with a letter. Next day he showed up with a dog...

NARRATOR: What kind of dog...?

MRS BRIMLEY: One of them kind, like before...

NARRATOR: A spaniel... must be one of the seven.

MRS BRIMLEY: One's enough in this house, thank you very, it's already chewed a cushion...

The barking starts again. She jerks her head.

MRS BRIMLEY: He's in the garden. Imagine Mr Fisk in the garden. He'll be growing roses, next...

And the Narrator goes through and she goes back into the parlour.

54 INT. FISK'S HOUSE - STUDY - DAY

The Narrator comes into the study and goes over to the window where Fisk Sr can be seen with a young Cocker Spaniel which is running round and round in circles, its master clapping his hands in encouragement.

The Narrator watches a moment, his eyes bright. Then he turns, and TO THE CAMERA, says,

NARRATOR: That was the end of my talks with Dean Spanley, although my father sometimes saw

him at the club. I do not know what they
talked about, if anything...as for the question of
reincarnation, I resolved to wait and see, albeit
with more anticipation than hitherto...

*And then back to the GARDEN and we see the dog jumping up
in excitement and Fisk stroking it and OVER THIS:*

NARRATOR (V.O.): ...And should I find myself in
the form of a dog, I trust I will be so fortunate as
to belong to a master as kind as my father...

*And we FREEZE FRAME on the dog leaping into Fisk Sr's
arms.*

THE END

A TRICK OF THE TALE:
ADAPTING LORD DUNSANY FOR THE SCREEN

I first read *My Talks With Dean Spanley* about twenty-five years ago and succumbed to its charm at a sitting. The Narrator's straight-faced parody of Karmic curiosity, insight into the mind of man's best friend, and a certain shaggy dog silliness blended perfectly. It was, as they say, my cup of tea. It wasn't immediately obvious to me that there was a script in it, or indeed that there was any need to try and translate it to another medium, so satisfactorily did it work in its own. It wasn't until, on holiday a few years after that, sated with Sienna and its umber glories, I made a first attempt to write a script from the novella. This was strictly for fun, the equivalent of a book you read on holiday to fill up the bits between meals and sight-seeing. I didn't trouble to enquire as to the availability or the copyright situation. It was done for the simple pleasure of working with Lord Dunsany's absurdist whimsy and seeing his characters walk around in my mind. When it was completed (it took about a week) it came out at around 50 pages and, with the exception of the very end, was a faithful transcription of the story.

Of course, it's all very well to write a script for the fun of it, but when you have the finished article in front of you it's inevitable that you start to think about its actualization in this new incarnation. At 50 pages, however, the only outlet was possibly television and one-hour, stand-alone movies were not in great demand. And *Spanley* had, from a production point of view, the disadvantage of needing a considerable amount of dog footage to make it work. The old adage, never work with dogs or children, has been triumphantly ignored on many occasions, but it still, in this case, added a dimension of unpredictability to what otherwise was a fairly straightforward adaptation. For it was clear, from the first pass, that this was a piece actors could wear like a well-cut suit. Generations of British thespians have absorbed the particular grammar of such portrayals and the nuances of the underlying humour. At this point there were only three characters: the Narrator, Spanley and Wrather. The form was a series of two and three-handed scenes, with the Narrator's voice-over making the linkages and the whole interspersed with the dog stuff, which from the outset was conceived as being human-free. The only concession to the medium was that rather than the tale tapering off into the classic Shaggy Dog ending, something a little more climactic was introduced that would bring a certain emotional closure, while also building up Wrather's part.

However, no one to whom I showed the script was much interested. Charming, droll, eccentric, were some of the responses, but no takers. This was all back in the late eighties and after a few such comments I put it away, feeling I was still ahead of the game simply by having had a good time in the writing process. Screenwriters become, if not inured, certainly used to the reality that the ratio of screenplays to movies is hovering around a thousand to one. If you've been in the business as long as I have, you have piles of unproduced screenplays lying around. *Dean Spanley* joined a sizeable raft of such and passed out of mind. FADE TO BLACK: LEGEND: (ALMOST) 20 YEARS LATER:

Sometime in 2006 I got a call from a producer, one Matthew Metcalfe. He is a New Zealander and had come upon *Spanley* by a circuitous route that's worth sketching, if only to show that sometimes serendipity rules.

Matthew knew a man called Noel Trevarthan, also a Kiwi and an actor. Noel was the kind of actor who could have played the Narrator, or Spanley, for that matter, and had, in fact, worked in Britain and the United States quite extensively. He had shown Matthew a copy of the script several years earlier.

It had come into Noel's possession by virtue of the fact that he and I both lived on Kawau Island in New Zealand, and knew each other from conversations on the ferry that connects the island with the mainland. In the course of these talks, I mentioned the script and subsequently gave him a copy to read. This was more a social exchange than any kind of business thing. Truth was, I had long given up the notion of making a film from this script. I just thought it would amuse Noel. As it did.

So, Matthew's call came out of the blue. I hadn't spoken to Noel in a long time, several years, and in that interim he had, sadly, passed away. But

Matthew remembered the script and wanted to know its status. I told him it had no status and he, in turn, asked me if I was interested in reviving it. Which, from a producer means, will you do more work on it? I should say that I am not averse to such requests. The energy a new mind brings to old material is a significant element in the development process. But I felt fairly certain that *My Talks With Dean Spanley* was pretty much what it was, a short film; while Matthew envisaged a feature-length theatrical release. To even get into that ballpark, the script would have to be extended by 40-odd pages, almost one hundred percent of the present length. I felt that the soufflé would collapse, the custard would be over-egged, and the lily gilded by any such enlargement. And so it proved.

My first rewrite came to around 70 pages and it achieved that gain by expanding the role of the Nawab and giving him his cricketing eccentricities, and by just having more Narrator–Spanley scenes. It was not a successful solution. Still well short of feature length, it laboured at maintaining interest in the core dialogue exchanges between the Narrator and Spanley and it made the ending seem even more of an add-on than before.

Under Matthew's prompting I wrote another draft which inched the page count up, but didn't do the story any favours. A bit of me felt we were missing the point in trying to bulk it up, but it was also clear that minus that, the thing wouldn't fly.

In my line of work, I am frequently asked to write scripts from existing material, mostly novels, sometimes real life events, and, to make a distinction, historical incidents and characters. Invariably in these exercises the first task is to get rid of large amounts of material. Even your medium-length novel, say 250 to 300 pages, contains a lot more than can be got into your average movie length, which at 1½ hours is about 110 pages of screenplay. The adaptor's task is to cut judiciously and patch the gaps where cutting has occurred, while trying to retain the qualities the book possesses in its own right. The process is one fraught with dangers as anyone who has seen a film version of a favourite book can attest. But it is, by and large, a necessary process. You just can't get into a script, or a film, much of what a novel deals with in its medium. Landscape descriptions, internal mental processes, philosophical digressions, poetic diction, physical descriptions of characters, metaphor and image – all these are unwelcome in the screenplay.

Dialogue, story and setting are what the screen-writer deals with, and not much more.

In the case of *Dean Spanley*, the problem wasn't that material had to be excised. It was that there wasn't enough leg to fill the stocking. To make this glider fly the distance, it would be necessary to invent an engine in the form of another story-line to which the existing one could be attached. This is where adaptation ethics comes in. While it is all right, because unavoidable, to cut, it's a different business entirely to add. Ethics may be too lofty a term, but aesthetics is not. *Dean Spanley* worked perfectly in its original form. Would that be the case if a whole new plot was invented and inserted?

Which, of course, led to the question of what the new material would consist of. Between us, Matthew and I had come up with the idea that we would have to give the Narrator a more dramatically satisfactory reason for his interest in the Dean. The conceit that I proposed was that the Narrator would have a Father whose dog Spanley had been. This, while in keeping with the whimsy of the original, demanded a change in tone, one that steered the new script on a dangerous course. For Matthew felt that the father–son relationship and the estrangement between them should be what the film was about and that in the course of its telling these two should effect a genuine reconciliation and that the father should come to terms with not just the long-ago loss of his beloved dog, but also with the more recent and tragic loss of his other son in the Boer War.

While these were my suggestions, their implementation filled me with deep misgivings. There are different ways to describe the difficulties I foresaw. Mainly, it would be like introducing Chekov into Gilbert and Sullivan. Could anyone take seriously a man working through denial and grief for the loss of a child while talking to a Dean who, while inebriated, could remember being a Spaniel? How was the key change from whimsy to pathos to be accomplished, and would an audience, hopefully chuckling along with all this harmless malarkey, be inclined to, or capable of, tearing up at the moment of truth when Fisk Sr. recognizes Dean Spanley as his long lost pooch and, in the process, finds the capacity to grieve for his dead son?

My own belief was, not likely. The new material worked a treat in terms of bringing the script up to size, and the character of Fisk Sr., the major piece of invention, worked perfectly as an irascible, eccentric English gentleman. But nothing I was able to write convinced me that this wasn't a mixed metaphor, a joke that turned sententious and possibly sentimental; and this apprehension stayed with me through the various drafts and the gradual gathering of resources and momentum as Matthew took the script around the financial institutions on which any independent production depends. Even when director Toa Fraser came on board and it began to look as if, against very considerable odds, the project would get funded, I never lost my fear that it just wouldn't work, that the shift required would destroy the previous audience mood. But at the end of the day, a script is not an autonomous creation. It depends for its reality on a host of other talents and skills, the most important of which is the collaboration of actor and director.

So, since there was nothing else to be done, I decided to leave it to those elements to provide what I as the writer could not: to, in the time-honoured phrase, "lend an air of verisimilitude to an otherwise bald and unconvincing narrative". This abdication of responsibility was made more forgivable when the casting was complete, particularly with regard to Fisk Sr. For we would depend almost entirely on this performance to bring the audience from one realm to the other. Only if you believe, first, the comic excesses of the character, and then, second, accept his conversion to grieving parent and dog lover, would we get out of our little fable intact. It is no disrespect to any of the other members of the cast to say that this ambition came within reach when Peter O'Toole accepted the part. It is not for me to say more, save that his performance, for this viewer at any rate, resolved the dilemma created by the writer, and along with the other members of the ensemble, saved his blushes. Should I ever encounter Lord Dunsany in the Elysian Fields or wherever it is he walks his celestial dogs, my apologies for trying to embellish his lovely little tale will be made with the hope that he too might be persuaded by the liberties taken with his text when realized by such rich talents.

Sometimes you get lucky. *My Talks With Dean Spanley* represents the epitome of such good fortune in my career, and I would like to express my gratitude to all those who contributed to it along the way. Most especially to Matthew Metcalfe without whom, it is fair to say, the film would never

have been made. It is said that a producer is someone who knows a writer. This is one writer who has
known a fair few number of producers in his time,
but, as I said, sometimes you get lucky.

Alan Sharp
New Zealand, 2008

A PRODUCER'S TAKE,
OR HOW WE MADE THE MOVIE...

An eccentric tale of an Anglican Dean who believes he once was a dog... So began my first pitches in early 2005 for the film that would become *Dean Spanley*.

As any reasonable reader would probably concede, it was a proposal that was just begging for at best a raised eyebrow and, at worst, a flat no. Which is, of course, what I received the first time I mentioned this project to anyone.

I can still remember it now...

'A Dean who thinks he was a *what*? – pass, thanks.'

Now, it must be admitted that this is the film business where rejection is a part of everyday life, if not the norm. Nonetheless, a few too many Nos early on can doom any project to the Dante's Inferno of the movie world, development hell.

So, while my first was likely to be the first of many, I decided that this was a film that needed a different path. A path that would need tens of millions of dollars, but which (at least in the year 2005) did not look likely to be attracting the cheque writers of Hollywood by any stretch of a producer's considerable imagination.

Nevertheless, as the book you are holding reveals, the film did get made, and there is a story to tell of how it did. So, like any good after-dinner tale, it is perhaps best to go back and begin at the beginning.

For my part, it all really began one night back in late 2004 as I was drifting off to sleep. As the reader will learn from Alan Sharp's description of the development process, I had come across the short film version of the screenplay by way of a mutual friend in 1998 and had loved it from the opening lines to the final scene. However, there was little I could do with a 50-page screenplay, so like many wonderful ideas in this business it went into the bottom drawer where it would stay until a fateful night's sleep several years later.

That particular night in question I recall sitting bolt upright in my bed, in what might be called a 'Eureka!' moment, and thinking to myself, 'Dean Spanley – I must make it'. More importantly than that I had an idea as to how to make it work as a feature film. Of course, it must be pointed out that the path from 'Eureka' to 'Camera Set – Action' is a long and arduous one, but like all producers this one is an eternal optimist with, at times, what must seem to others an almost foolish level of enthusiasm. Thus what came next was somewhat typical of the species.

Leaping out of bed I headed for the bottom drawer of my desk where the (short) screenplay that filled my head with possibility was meant to reside. After some five years it was, of course, not there, which led (as it does at 1.00am) to the house being pulled to pieces in a fruitless effort to find this wondrous script of which I had such a clear vision (or so I thought at 1.00am that morning). By 4.00am my vision had somewhat been replaced by the sight of my house, which looked like a train wreck. The script was nowhere to be found, with only my cat left untouched, its disdain for what I had done to its sleeping area showing all over its little face.

Now, I will not bore the reader with the arcane detail of what came next, for it is enough to say that it took several months to even get a copy of the script and then begin to convince Alan Sharp that it should be further developed. Lots of phone calls and emails were exchanged, comprising the boring stuff of producing that I suspect no reader really wants to wade into. Suffice to say that eventually a partnership of sorts was found and Alan and I began the process of turning his short film screenplay into a full-blown feature film.

So it was that by early 2006 *Dean Spanley* was nicely making the transition to its soon to be fuller incarnation. However, this brings us back to the problem of how to pitch such a film and beyond that, how to get it funded.

Early attempts had, as previously described, not met with a particularly strong response. The message being clear that dogs who reincarnate as Deans was just not of the same sort of box office material as trucks and cars who transform into robots.

So as this next stage of development continued I took what was upon reflection the best possible course of action: I hid the project from the world.

Now this will, of course, seem (quite logically, I would argue) to the reader rather the wrong thing to do. After all, should not all producers be out there telling the world of their next masterpiece, whipping financiers into a state of frenzied anticipation and generally acting in a manner of supreme confidence and assuredness? Well, in this case, the answer is an unequivocal no. This was a project that could not show its face to the world until it was in nothing short of a solid state. Financiers would have to swoon at the story's charms and become infatuated by the cast possibilities that the film's roles promised if this was ever to be a 'go' film. So for nearly a year (most of 2006), while the writer worked quietly away, I busied myself with post-production on my then-current film, all the while hoping that what was simmering away in the writer's mind was to be nothing short of a stunning and exotic dish.

I had high hopes and my mind, I must confess, was filled with the imaginings of all producers, a film with stars, red carpets and glowing reviews. One can imagine then the anticipation I felt when in late 2006 a large envelope containing the script was handed to me by the writer. Each page was fantastic, with every flick of the page the story ever more potent and compelling as I had hoped it might be. Until, that is, I got to page 75…

Now, it's not that page 75 wasn't any good; it's simply that it was not there. Nor was page 76, 77 or 78, for that matter. The script just finished, incomplete.

Scripts arriving incomplete is, within the industry, something of an urban myth. One of those stories like finding a mouse in your Big Mac that many have heard of, but never actually experienced themselves. At this point it's important to clarify that Alan Sharp is one hell of a writer and not himself to be confused with those who would put a rodent in a burger. So I did what all producers would in this situation, I grabbed the phone and dialled. The conversation of which went something like this:

Writer: 'Hello.'

Producer: 'The script's fantastic, I love it…'

Note: Producers are excitable beasts and when faced with a fantastic screenplay are prone to skipping the formalities.

Writer: 'Great, great, I'm quite pleased with it myself.'

Producer: 'I enjoyed every page right up to the point where it stopped.'

Writer: 'Right, right.'

Producer: 'So I think we should finish the screenplay.'

Writer: 'Right...' (followed by a long pause)

Truth be told, the conversation was a little more than the above, with much discussion about what the end of the film would be. Either way, Alan agreed to keep writing and within a few days a shiny new screenplay, very similar to the one printed in this book, was delivered to me. It was, in short, a beautiful and moving piece of writing and it deserved to be brought to the screen. It just needed a director, money and cast.

Of course, producers don't make films by themselves and, for that matter, they rarely produce films on their own. For the previous two years I had been working with an excellent London-based producer called Alan Harris and it was to him that I first turned with the now-finished script for *Dean Spanley*. Luckily for the project he loved it and so this skilled producer now became part of the conspiracy to let the right people see the project at the right time.

Collectively (now there were two producers trying to make this movie happen) the first thought was of course who shall direct this? Choosing the director of a movie is one of the most difficult and important decisions a producer will make along the path towards production. Get it right and glory is yours, get it wrong and you will see all your dreams come undone before your eyes. My own view was that we needed someone who understood family, who got the subtext of the powerful emotions that exist between father and son, and who could understand that a whimsical story about an eccentric Dean who thought he was once a dog could become a metaphor for the powerful forces that the film would explore.

Both Alan Harris and I thought that a New Zealand director called Toa Fraser could well fit the description above. He had directed only one other film before (*No. 2*) but it had won the Audience Award at the Sundance Film Festival in 2006 and had shown a real flair for storytelling, family, pathos and imagery. Further to that, Toa had an established international reputation as a playwright, something that we felt would help qualify him to breathe life into scenes that in many cases were static, taking place in a room, club or other such confined space. He was our first choice and I hope that when you, the reader, see the film, you will agree that not only was he the best choice, but that he also brought a special magic to the film.

Signing a director does not, of course, put your film instantly into production (unless it is Mr Spielberg or Mr Lucas that you have just signed), you still have to go through the boring, but unfortunately completely necessary part of financing the film. Now, given that this introduction is to a book that hopefully the reader will enjoy over a glass of something while sitting by the fire, and given that the subject of financing leaves even those who work in the business with eyes glazing at just the mention of the word, we will leave this part of the process out of our description. Suffice to say that the New Zealand Film Commission, Aramid Entertainment, Screen East and Lip Sync Productions all felt that a Dean who gets drunk then reminisces about being a dog was as suitable a subject as any to pour millions of dollars into.

The reader may recall at this point that the script was previously described as hidden from the world, for reasons that suggest that those who were trying to make this film were somewhat insane or at the very least delusional. Be that as it may, at some point it must be revealed to the wider film world and it was with this in mind that we as producers gingerly began to show the script in early 2007. The plan was to let just a few people at a time read it, allowing each to enjoy it and have the wonderful premise behind it find a place in their heart. One by one Alan Harris and I did this, building the script up in the financing community and allowing the word of mouth that this was something special to find its way out to those who can make the green-light decisions. All of this was aided by the prodigious talent of Toa Fraser, whose win the previous year at Sundance ensured that all who considered the project saw it as we intended it to be seen, as nothing short of the highest quality drama with a unique, fresh and original story to tell. This path proved the right one and over a period of some six months *Dean Spanley* became known as an exciting and original film with a genuine future in theatres everywhere. This was confirmed when our first distribution partners, Alliance Films in Canada and Paramount in Australasia, came on board. From that point on, the script was very much un-hidden and was, as Wrather's Aunt Molly would say, 'a boat that was going to float'.

There is, of course, so much more to making a movie and in some way I am sure that I am doing the enthusiastic film reader a disservice by not continuing with my description of the path to production of this movie. But, truth be told, it would fill a book on its own to describe the adventures, trials and tribulations involved as we banked the millions (ready to spend again on the film), cast the actors and hired the crew ready to roll camera. Instead, by the time the reader casts their eyes over these short passages they will be able to see for themselves how well the project worked out and whether the choice of cast, director, locations, costumes, music and all the other cornucopia of resources that go into a movie were the right ones. Certainly this producer hopes that the answer will be a resounding yes.

The process of making any movie is a special one and it will be for the rest of my life that I remember such a team as came together to tell this lovely story. Thus I hope the reader will indulge me as I take this rather public opportunity to thank my fellow co-producer, Alan Harris, the film's director Toa Fraser, the entire cast and crew, the financiers and last but very far from least, the film's writer, Alan Sharp. A man for whom I have the utmost respect and affection and without whom there would be no retelling for the screen of this great classic of which you the reader are now in possession. *My Talks with Dean Spanley* by Edward John Moreton Drax Plunkett, 18th Baron of Dunsany.

Matthew Metcalfe
Soho, London 2008

DIRECTING THE DEAN

When *Dean Spanley* first came into my life I was – to quote Peter O'Toole – shaking like a Sheffield dog shitting penknives. It was December, in a year that for me had started in the snow at the Sundance Film Festival, with the premiere of my first film, *No. 2.* I had spent the rest of the year following it around the world – Tokyo! New York! Taipei! London! – promoting it and probably going to too many parties.

I had sworn – I swear about such things, foolishly – I'd go to no more parties but it was at that very one, the last one, the one I almost didn't go to, that I met producer Matthew Metcalfe, and whether by happenstance, coincidence or significance, stepped into the curious and exhilarating world of *Dean Spanley*.

Matthew pitched it to me as a story about a Dean who used to be a dog, which sounded interesting enough and it was through that lens that I began reading Alan Sharp's screenplay. The audacious twist of the script, though, is that while it wears its shaggy dog whimsy on its sleeve, at its heart it's a story about a father and a son, and what it takes to bring family together.

I was flattered that Matthew had the courage and insight to ask me to direct. *No. 2* is a contemporary story, set in a working-class suburb of Auckland, about a gin-swilling Fiji matriarch who rules the roost over her large Pacific Island family and who orders a feast on the hottest day of the year. It's a story distanced from *Dean Spanley* by more than oceans and centuries. The common language of the two stories, however, is family.

There were other things that I was drawn to in the script: I loved Alan's bold celebration of the English language, the way it was crammed full of memorable lines. I was excited about the setting: England in the early years of the twentieth century, when the country was having a full-on conversation with the rest of the world. I knew, for instance, that the first All Black team to tour England arrived in 1905. And I was born and grew up in England, so for me the film became a homecoming of sorts.

I also had an instinctive connection to the spiritual dilemma of the story. I had grown up in a picture postcard Hampshire village, with its medieval church at the centre of the community. When I was a boy, clambering around the *de rigueur* moss-swathed village gravestones, my Fiji-born father would speak of ghosts and Pacific myth; recount supernatural stories in very real terms. It's common in my Pacific family – and has been, over generations – to worship at the Catholic church in the morning, go home, eat, drink, and consider the current form of your lamented relatives. It is a generally accepted fact that my grandmother showed up at her own wake in the form of a heron. Indeed, the only dissenting argument states that the heron was not my grandmother, but my uncle. These things are a matter of fact in the Pacific. Maybe because he's a Scotsman or maybe because he spends half his life on an island in the South Pacific, Alan's script spoke to that sensibility despite the story's English trappings.

I had a series of meetings with Matthew and Alan – on the aforementioned island, memorably, with prosciutto and melon, and vichyssoise soup – and we threw around ideas of casting and locations. Quite early on we thought it would be great if Wrather – originally conceived as a Scotsman – were to be an Australian, the kind of guy that had somehow made his way to England and may or may not have killed a man in Borneo en route. He had to be played by Bryan Brown. Sam Neill, too, was always part of our initial conversations, and our first choice to play Dean Spanley. I knew Sam a little bit, sensed he had a rock and roll edge we hadn't yet seen on screen and was intrigued by the idea of him taking a character we seem to think he's played before – the Dean – and subverting it with something a bit more soulful-slash-funky – the Dog. Sam was not so easily persuaded, and turned the film down three times before he figured out how he might be able to do it.

The struggle in any project, and of course in life, is figuring out your voice. And while the early ideas were exciting, my anxieties about the film were all to do with the family at the core of the story, and their home. Homes are important to me. *No. 2* was named after a house. With that film, I knew the very street we had to film on even before I had begun writing the screenplay. With *Dean Spanley*, Alan had written a script that could take place in any town in England. The opening stanzas suggested Bath or Brighton to me but those towns didn't seem quite right. I had grown up near Portsmouth, and given that I was into the idea of showing an England with an international vibe, a port town seemed like a good idea. But it seemed too open and flat and again, not right. I toured around all over the country, trying, unsuccessfully, to find a home for the story.

Things began to fall into place when production designer Andrew McAlpine and locations man Paul O'Grady came on board and we headed to the East of England. The town of Wisbech in Cambridgeshire was a bustling trading town at the time of the story, and incredibly much of the architecture is unchanged. It has a vigorous, working-money edge and a kind of sandstone, continental buzz that suited the tastes of McAlpine and me down to the very ground we were pounding. Yet as we swarmed around the streets pointing cameras like a triumvirate of art-school stormtroopers, I became increasingly nervous that the producers – Metcalfe and Alan Harris, following at an uncomfortable distance, only just out of earshot when the wind changed – were sensing what I was beginning to believe myself: that I had no idea how to make this movie.

The jewel in the crown of Wisbech, though, as Paul O'Grady very well knew, is Peckover House, a

National Trust home perfect for our means, not only architecturally, but also in that its walls seemed all touched by real people, by family. We read about and looked at images of the Peckover family, the Quaker, banking descendants of Dutch settlers. We were inspired by the idea that Roland Penrose, the surrealist painter and poet, who counted Man Ray and Picasso as his mates and Lee Miller as his wife, was the grandson of Lord Peckover. We began to envisage the Fisks Jr. and Sr. as similar characters. It was a breakthrough moment: from the state house of *No. 2* to this stately home in Wisbech, I sat out on the back steps of Peckover House and surveyed the backyard. We spent the rest of the week in the region. We went for early-morning swims at windswept Brancaster, ate local samphire, drank some award-winning Elgood's bitter and realised *Dean Spanley* had found its home. It was a beginning.

Peter O'Toole is a man who knows about beginnings and endings. Moments before a take, when he's found his mark, when the camera's rolling and the clapper-loader claps the board, he lets out a roar that to me sounds like he's opening a channel between him and the gods of Drama; like moving from the mortal world to the spirit world. If you're standing a metre in front of him, right by the camera – the best place to direct – this can be a scary thing. As my 1st AD Stuart Renfrew says, "When you step in front of the camera with these guys, you're stepping into the lion's den, man." He said it as a warning; I like to whisper a direction in an actor's ear, so it's the last thing they think of. I had previously directed one movie. O'Toole had previously won eight Oscar nominations, and gone toe-to-toe with Katherine Hepburn, Richard Burton, Omar Sharif, Alec Guinness, Elizabeth Taylor. I love the scene in *The Lion in Winter* when he beats up Timothy Dalton with words: 'You're not very good at this, are you, boy. Use all your voices! When I bellow, you bellow back!' Our assembled cast between them had worked with Spielberg, Mamet, Bertolucci, Lumet, Donaldson, Beresford. Quite early in the shoot, O'Toole called me into his green room. Slightly out of breath, a little unsteady on his feet, he put his hands on my shoulders: 'I'm going to teach you something. That David Lean taught me. Actors will love you for it.' You better listen when you get that kind of advice.

We were all intimidated by scene forty-eight, the climactic dinner scene. Eighteen pages (movie-making wisdom suggests that should equate to eighteen *minutes*) in one room, and much of it dialogue that Sam Neill had to learn. We feared it. We shot it over five days, in an exhausting, emotion- and concentration-sapping test match of a shoot. And Sharp's script is unrelenting – just when you're done sculpting comedy and drama out of that behemoth, you're into the hallway for another three days of delicate performance in the aftermath of the dinner. We shot on digital, so we were unafraid to go for very long takes – sometimes as long as seven minutes. You have to hone your concentration on the actors for every second of each take. When that set-up's done, you have to rush to figure out where to place the camera next. It's tough, athletic work. But between takes you play the ukulele and throw the rugby ball around. Jeremy Northam and Peter O'Toole were as keen to kick the ball around a backyard in Wisbech as Rene Naufahu and Xavier Horan were in Mt. Roskill on *No. 2.*

The shoot is hard work and great fun; the cutting room is just hard work. Months in a basement in Soho, in winter, locked in a room with one another guy. Lucky the other guy was my mate Chris Plummer, who had cut *No. 2.* I was lucky on

Dean Spanley to have a key off-sider every step of the way: Andrew McAlpine, the London-based New Zealander who had designed, amongst other things, *The Piano* and *Clockers*; Leon Narbey, my friend and mentor from *No. 2*, one of New Zealand's most respected film artists; Stuart Renfrew, straight-talking, kite-surfing, vastly experienced 1st AD; and Don McGlashan, who wrote most of his score from a tour bus crossing the States with Crowded House. He wrote his exquisite 'Dream Dreams You' for scene 48 sitting next to the bus driver at midnight on the New Jersey turnpike. But no matter how good your mates are, the cutting room is hard.

There you finally nail the voice of the story. Before we went in, I got a call from Chris, around Christmas time. He was travelling around France, thinking about the story. He called to say, "I think you should get a shot of the dead brother." I thought it was a bad idea. I went back to New Zealand to film some dogs running around in fields. But I was haunted by the images we had shot in England. When I closed my eyes I would see the shot of O'Toole imagining his dead son. I was at the beach, with my girlfriend, it was summertime, we had heads full of sand and salt water... I was struck by how cold, how formal and dressed-up everything we had shot in England was. I hadn't known how I wanted to shoot the dogs before but now it was obvious we needed that footage to be epic, colourful and above all sensual. It also became clear that Chris was right: we needed that shot of the soldier, an image that contrasted with what Alan Sharp describes as O'Toole's wan, wasted face as he remembers his son, something that spoke of masculinity and lost youth and family.

If we were going to do right by Alan's script, we felt the film had to be about something more than dogs running around the countryside.

I've said that *Dean Spanley* became a homecoming of sorts. It also feels like a goodbye. We asked Xavier Horan to play O'Toole's late son. Xavier was one of the least experienced actors on *No. 2* but casting director Di Rowan said he had movie star written all over him (and she can pick 'em – see Anna Paquin and Keisha Castle-Hughes). Like *No. 2*, like my Pacific family, Xavier is an exuberant, handsome, athletic, charming, Youth… Here, now, in London, like Fisk Sr., I'm haunted by the image of him lying supine in the grasslands of the Southern Hemisphere. Beginnings and endings.

Late in post-production, Peter O'Toole came into the sound studio to record a little extra dialogue. He opened up the channel to the gods one more time and barked into the microphone, 'You're easily pleased is all I can say.' Like that, one take, and we were out, back into the mortal world, the most mortal streets of Soho. We walked a bit, talked. I got a potted history of Soho and the world according to Peter O'Toole. We had a jar, talked rugby. He told me I'd like Lawrence Dallaglio. "He's a man. Doesn't like any fuss." He finished his glass and was gone.

I reflected on two gentle, joyous hours spent in the company of one of the greats, a direct descendant of Shakespeare and Burbage. I reflected on the gift of *Dean Spanley*, the curious tale that made it to the screen by such circuitous means. I reflected on lost family. I finished my glass, and just for a moment, sat still.

Toa Fraser
London, 2008

CREDITS

The NEW ZEALAND FILM COMMISSION in association with
SCREEN EAST CONTENT INVESTMENT FUND,
ARAMID ENTERTAINMENT and LIP SYNC PRODUCTIONS LLP
presents a MATTHEW METCALFE/ATLANTIC FILM
GROUP PRODUCTION

Jeremy NORTHAM Sam NEILL Bryan BROWN and Peter O'TOOLE
in *"Dean Spanley"* with Judy PARFITT Art MALIK

Casting Dan HUBBARD *Make-Up* Marese LANGAN
Costume Designer Odile DICKS-MIREAUX
Line Producer Liz BUNTON *Original Music by* Don McGLASHAN
Production Designer Andrew McALPINE
Director of Photography Leon NARBEY *Editor* Chris PLUMMER
Executive Producers Simon FAWCETT Finola DWYER David PARFITT
and Alan SHARP

Based on the novel *"My Talks With Dean Spanley"* by Lord DUNSANY
Written by Alan SHARP *Produced by* Matthew METCALFE Alan HARRIS
Directed by Toa FRASER

www.deanspanleymovie.com